Love ~~NOTEBOOK~~

NEVER-ending KISS

"Don't worry – I've got somewhere in mind that I think you'll like," Luke went on, to her relief. Then he kissed her again, still very gently, his hand reaching under her mass of hair to find her neck. His touch was electric. Jess could feel herself trembling.

"Good night, firebrand," whispered Luke. "See you soon." That night, as she fell at last into a feverish sleep, Jess began to dream that she was diving from a high rock into a vast lake, and something was telling her that she was about to plunge in far too deep.

Love ~~NOTEBOOK~~ NOTEBOOK

NEVER-ending KISS

Amber Vane

SCHOLASTIC

Scholastic Children's Books
An imprint of Scholastic Ltd
Euston House, 24 Eversholt Street
London, NW1 1DB, UK
Registered office: Westfield Road, Southam, Warwickshire, CV47 0RA
SCHOLASTIC and associated logos are trademarks and or
registered trademarks of Scholastic Inc.

First published as *Hopelessly Devoted* by Scholastic Publications Ltd, 1995
This edition published in the UK by Scholastic Ltd, 2009

Text copyright © Amber Vane, 1995

ISBN 978 1407 11156 8

British Library Cataloguing-in-Publication Data
A CIP catalogue record for this book is available
from the British Library

The right of Amber Vane to be identified as the author of this work
has been asserted by her.

Printed in the UK by CPI Bookmarque, Croydon, CR0 4TD
Papers used by Scholastic Children's Books are made from wood grown
in sustainable forests.

1 3 5 7 9 10 8 6 4 2

www.scholastic.co.uk/zone

One

The stage was in darkness. An expectant hush filled the air. Then a single spotlight picked out a lone figure. It was Jess's big moment.

For twenty minutes the band had been pelting out their usual wild brand of indie-rock. "Not exactly heavy metal," Thomas, the bass player, would say. "More sort of aluminium, our style is."

"Crushable, recyclable, very green," Jess would add.

"Don't forget the touch of brass." That was Ellie, Jess's best friend, who played saxophone and was always trying to get the rest of them to show some interest in jazz.

The four members of *Species* had been friends for so long that they practically talked in code. If Jess or Ellie thought a boy was a bit of a nerd they always called him a Dylan, because of a really sad case who'd been in their class at primary school. Ben, the drummer, would occasionally complain of having a bad case of the Number 29s. That meant his parents were giving him a hard time, and dated back to the week when he and Thomas had had a competition to see who could be most irritating to their families. Ben had proudly scored 29 different shouting matches in a single week and was still reigning champion.

Now the four had left school and had just started A level courses at the Sixth Form College in Amberley, a small town near Birmingham where they all lived. And tonight they were making their college debut at the Saturday night talent evening.

"Talent!" Ben had exclaimed in disgust. "What a naff idea! You won't catch me plonking around some kiddy hall doing my party piece for a bunch of losers with nowhere better to go than some spotty teenage version of Butlins. Out of season."

Thomas had sighed, his freckled nose wrinkling in consternation, a worried frown on his slightly plump, slightly comical face.

"Yes, well, it's OK for you to scoff," he'd reasoned. "Clever scientists don't really need to be performers, do they. You only need to know how, not why."

It was a familiar argument. Ben and Ellie were good at science, Thomas and Jess at the arts, and their slanging matches about which was more useful had intensified now

2

because Ben had got such brilliant GCSEs that the others were secretly in awe of him and felt it was their duty to put him down as much as possible to prevent him getting too smug.

Thomas had managed to persuade Ben that he owed it to his friends to turn up at the talent-spotting evening, even though the college had misguidedly called it "Reach for the Stars" so Ben had instantly dubbed it "Topple Over and Die". Jess had long thought that Ben had to act hard and cynical because he was physically so weedy that if a football came flying in his direction and someone yelled, "*Kick!*" he'd blink behind his glasses and say, "Why?" with a puzzled look on his face.

But Ben was a good friend. He knew it was important for the others to make an impact in the first week. Jess was taking Theatre Studies and Music for A levels, and Thomas was doing Theatre Studies, Music and ICT, so they both wanted to take part in as many performances as they could, and for that they needed to be seen. Ellie couldn't have cared less about being picked for shows. But she was just as keenly interested in being seen – preferably by as many boys as possible. Ellie regarded boys as her area of special interest and would have done A level flirting if she hadn't felt so qualified to teach it.

"Just think of the effect you're going to have on all the new girls," she'd pointed out cunningly to Ben. "It'll be your big chance to impress all the ones who don't know you yet. There

3

you'll be, beating the daylights out of all those drums with such masterful passion – they'll be falling over themselves to get near you."

Privately, Ben was rather hoping that she was right. He was shy with girls and usually covered his embarrassment by being very quiet and looking very bored. So although he pretended to be putting himself out to help the other members of the band, he was secretly pleased at the chance to shine without having to speak.

And it was fortunate that they had turned up. The theatre was packed, but not many students had come forward to offer their talents. There had been five attempts at stand-up comedy – brave rather than funny. Three girls had performed a few numbers as a singing trio, with their own backing track. And there had been a whole string of rappers, of course, some of them pretty good.

But there was no doubt as soon as *Species* took to the stage that they were the hit of the evening. Jess, dressed in a tight leather skirt , had beaten and whammed her guitar into wild, siren-like wails and screeching riffs for song after song. Responding to the appreciative yells from the audience, she'd stamped her black thigh boots up and down the stage, screaming out the lyrics in harmony with Ellie's searing saxophone.

They'd been through a few well-known chart numbers and

a few more songs Thomas had written for them. But the sound had been consistently loud, relentless and aggressive. Now there was silence. You could hear the audience wondering what was coming next. The spotlight was on Jess. Her dark, tangled hair had broken free of the knotted scarves that had tied it back and now framed her flushed face.

For a few seconds she stood quite still, her guitar hanging round her waist, her arms by her sides. Then she looked up and began to sing in a pure, sweet, unaccompanied contralto. It was an old Beatles number, "You Really Got a Hold on Me," but the way Jess was treating it, it might have been a hymn rather than a suggestive piece of rock and roll.

At the first chorus Ellie joined her in a close harmony, the two girls standing together. After the first electrifying verse the girls spun round, grabbed their instruments, and the whole band launched into hard rock once again.

There was thunderous applause, whistles, even screams. And then they were into their final number. This was Ben's cue for a dramatic drum solo – the one he was hoping would somehow give him a little much-needed sex appeal. Ellie and Jess managed to snatch a few moments to swap notes as he crashed into his crescendo.

"I feel as if my whole past is flashing before me," Ellie whispered. "I've already seen four people I've been out with . . . and three of them I was hoping I'd never see again."

Jess could barely hear her over Ben's frenzied crashes. But then, she wasn't really paying much attention. She was squinting out through the stage lights at a tall, attractive figure standing in the aisle very near the front. He was dark and good-looking with brooding eyes and a casual slouch. Jess saw that he was holding a notebook. She nudged Ellie.

"Look! A talent scout!" she hissed.

"Talk about talent!" Ellie smacked her lips appreciatively. "He's the only thing that comes close in the whole place."

The girls were so busy ogling him that they almost forgot their cues for the close of the number. Thomas had to remind Jess by kicking her subtly in the foot. But Thomas was never very subtle. His kick sent her reeling into Ellie, and the two of them nearly skittered right off the stage. They tried to pretend it was all part of the act, but Jess noticed the good-looking guy scribbling in his notebook, and somehow she was sure he'd noticed the mad scramble up on stage.

After the lights had come on and the show was over they were bombarded. Even Ben had attracted some interest, and was busily showing a couple of girls how to do a drum roll. Ellie, as usual, was surrounded by admirers. She was very blonde, very skinny and very pretty and never had trouble attracting boyfriends. It was getting rid of them that always caused her problems. Even now, the four exes were all somewhere in the circle round her and she was managing to chat to several others over the general chaos. Thomas was always very popular, too. Jess thought girls must like him because he wasn't a threat to them. He was great fun and very easy to get on with but with his boyish looks, rueful smile, freckles and solid build he wasn't exactly a turn-on. More of a brother figure.

Jess was about to join Thomas, who was laughing with a group of friends, when she felt a tap on her shoulder. She turned round and froze. It was as if the whole place had fallen silent and she was alone again in the spotlight. For there, standing right behind her, was the talent scout. Close up, he was even more gorgeous. He was very tanned with a strong, chiselled face and eyes which looked appraisingly straight at her.

"That was quite some performance," he said at once. "Especially the acrobatics at the end."

"Oh, I'm glad you enjoyed that," Jess answered as glibly as she could. "We practised it for ages."

"Your timing was magnificent," the talent scout went on. She still couldn't tell if he was joking. But she didn't care, either. She just wanted to carry on talking to him and feeling his eyes on her.

"I'm Luke Meade," he said, extending his hand to her.

"Jessica Mackenzie," she mumbled, aware only of the sensation of his firm hand shaking hers, then holding it just a little longer before releasing it. "Er . . . why have you been taking notes all evening?"

"Oh, I'm a reporter," he explained. "For the *Amberley Herald*. I thought I'd do a story on this 'Reach for the Stars' thing, but quite honestly it was a bit of a wash-out until you came on. I was just about to leave, actually."

"You mean – you're going to write about us? In the newspaper?" Jess was so keyed up with excitement that she forgot to look casual. Luke laughed.

"I might. I mean, it's not often you get a sexy singer and mean guitarist and brilliant gymnast all in one, is it?"

Jess looked dejected. Obviously he had noticed their undignified slip-up in that last number and he was going to make fun of them. But then he spoke again. "You really do have a great voice, you know. Do you always sing so aggressively? I would have thought you're much better suited to ballads – softer things."

"Oh, I do a bit of everything really," Jess answered vaguely. Her heart was beating wildly and she badly wanted to say something witty and clever to make him laugh, only her tongue seemed to be freezing up in her mouth. "When we're *Species* we tend to do the heavier stuff. But I'm interested in musicals and classic rock and a bit of country. My friend Ellie prefers jazz. And our bass player, Thomas – he's into weird contemporary stuff that he composes on computer."

"I'd love to hear you singing something gentler," Luke said, his voice sounding like a caress. "You've got a wonderful velvet quality."

Jess found herself becoming tongue-tied again and was furious. How come she could banter away for hours with practically anybody, but with the one decent-looking, half-way attractive guy she'd encountered all year she'd suddenly turned to jelly?

"Watch out for the smooth-talker," whispered a voice in her ear. It was Ben, sidling up behind her. "Any minute now he'll be trying to take you away from all this."

She swung round to glare at him. He was grinning. Thomas was with him.

"Come on, Jess – we're off to the bar before it closes."

Jess loved her friends dearly. But at that moment she wished they were on the other side of the planet. Why couldn't they just disappear and let her get on with being enchanted by this gorgeous stranger?

"You remind me of a singer called Grace Hari – do you know her?" Luke was saying. Know her! Grace Hari was a singer-songwriter who was just breaking into the big time with her own band. She was Jess's hero – especially as she had come from the same town.

Jess nodded enthusiastically. "I think she's great."

"I've got a couple of tickets to see her on tour next Saturday. Do you fancy coming?"

Jess nearly squeaked with joy. He was asking her out – on a dream date, to see her favourite singer. She tried to sound nonchalant. "Isn't she appearing in Coventry?" she asked.

"No problem," he answered airily. "We'll drive. I'll pick you up around seven and we'll be in plenty of time. OK?"

Jess floated after the others, and was still in a daze when Ellie handed her a Coke.

"So who was the talent scout?" Ellie demanded. "Looked like you were being spotted for something." Jess told the others who he was and Thomas gave a whistle.

"A reporter! Just you make sure you're nice to him, Jess, and do everything he says. Because if he gives us a good review it'll be the launch of our careers into stardom."

Jess wasn't listening. She was thinking about those dark, searching eyes, the feel of his hand closing round hers. And she was wondering how on earth she was going to get through the days and nights until she could be with him again.

Two

When Jess came down to earth the next day, she realized that her date with Luke was going to present a few problems. First of all, how was she going to persuade her mother to let her drive off to Coventry with a complete stranger?

"Tricky," agreed Ellie over the phone that morning. "It's a language problem really. We say cool, they say dangerous. We say exciting, they say . . ."

"Dangerous," supplied Jess with a sigh. "I think I'm going to have to start working on her right away."

"You've got practically a week," said Ellie hopefully. "You'll think of something. What are you going to wear?"

Jess sighed again. "That's my even worse problem. I don't know. What would you wear for the hottest date imaginable?"

Ellie considered. "Well, remember Oliver who bought me a drink last night? The OK-looking one with glasses? He's taking me to Space on Friday – you know, that new disco. I'll probably go shiny – my pink satin top, the one that shows lots of bare stomach. I like to drive them crazy."

Jess giggled. Ellie always knew how to cheer her up. But that didn't help her to solve any of her problems.

But she needn't have worried. The following evening the *Amberley Herald* carried Luke's account of the Sixth Form College talent night. He was disappointed in the general standard but raved about "the inventive student rock band *Species*, which stole the show." He didn't even allude to the fact that two members had very nearly rocketed off the stage. Best of all were his final remarks.

"There was some genuine raw musical promise here – I wasn't surprised to learn that several of the band are music students. The one to watch is the lead singer and guitarist Jessica Mackenzie who has yet to discover the right environment for her luscious voice."

"Oh, Jess!" breathed her mum proudly. "Fancy someone saying that about you – in the newspaper! I'm going to buy every copy. Gran would love one, and all the aunties . . ."

"Please, Mum!" protested Jess's younger brother Harry. "Don't let it go to her head even more than it has already, or she'll swell up and explode. Come on, Jess, confess. How much did you pay him?"

Jess was tempted to hit him, as she usually did when he

was irritating, which was about eighty per cent of the time. But he'd given her a cue that was just too convenient to miss.

"Actually, I didn't have to pay him," she said casually, "as long as I agreed to go out with him. He's taking me to see Grace Hari . . ."

It worked! Mum had already decided that he must be a charming young man to have written such lovely things about her daughter. She was even quite impressed that he was actually going to take her out in a car. Now Jess had to work out how she was going to make it through the rest of the week without bursting.

By Saturday evening she'd worked herself up to fever pitch. She spent hours getting ready, threading red and silver beads into her long, tangly curls. She'd decided to wear her favourite tight black jeans with a sexy red-and-black top borrowed from Ellie. It flashed with beads and sequins and showed off her stomach – Ellie's favourite area.

When the front door bell rang, she crept downstairs nervously. If Mum saw her she was bound to disapprove. She'd never actually said: "You're not going out like that!" but this could always be the first time. She managed to get to the door undetected, but when she opened it, there was Thomas lounging on the step. He looked her up and down gravely, then said: "You're never going out like that!"

"What do you mean?" Jess snapped crossly. "Since when have you been a prude? And anyway, what are you doing here?"

"Very nice, Miss Hospitality," sniffed Thomas. "You certainly know how to make a boy feel wanted. In answer to your questions, I think I'll take them backwards. I'm here to sort out a little software problem with your resident genius." Jess remembered that Thomas and Harry were working together on some complicated computer game. One of the most irritating things about her brother was that he was so good at things like that.

"As for being a prude," Thomas went on, "I think you're missing the point. Look, Jess, you're going out with a nice guy, right? You want to impress him, right? You want to look sophisticated, right?" Jess nodded, wondering what he was leading up to. "So why – why are you dressed up like a Barbie doll? This outfit qualifies you for the cover of *Sugar*. And that, by the way, is what I mean."

He followed her into the house, picking an apple from the fruit dish as he went. "OK," conceded Jess. "What do you suggest, since you've just appointed yourself my personal style consultant?"

Thomas looked at her carefully for a few moments. "Have you got a black jacket? A shiny one, preferably."

Jess didn't have one, but she knew someone who did. She raced up to her mother's wardrobe and reappeared a few minutes later wearing a soft white shirt with a black silk jacket. "How does it look?" she asked anxiously.

Thomas shook his head. "Take it off."

Jess panicked. "Make your mind up!" she said crossly. "I thought you said I needed a jacket."

"I did," Thomas said calmly. "Take the shirt off. Then put the jacket back on."

The minute Jess tried his idea she admitted, reluctantly, that he was right. The jacket looked great with nothing underneath, falling softly over her tight jeans. And when Luke turned up a few minutes later, she could tell from his appreciative gaze that the look was perfect.

His car was a battered Peugeot that rattled worryingly as soon as he got into fifth gear.

"It's a bit noisy," he shouted above the roar of the engine, "but it's all I can afford at the moment." He explained that he was working for the paper for a year before going to university. "I do quite a lot of routine work in the office and whenever I can I try to do some reporting. They usually let me do the rock music because I'm the only person there who's actually been to any gigs since Bob Dylan toured England. The first time."

Jess laughed and began to relax. Luke was great company, and kept her in fits with his stories about working at the newspaper.

"Obituaries are the worst," he said. "People can be so

unreasonable about them. I had to edit two the other day. One was about a woman who'd set up the first local family planning clinic about a hundred years ago and the other was about some Baroness who kept a bird sanctuary. It wasn't my fault the pictures got mixed up . . ."

By the time they'd taken their seats in the auditorium Jess was beginning to feel she was in a dream. Luke was gorgeous-looking, he was fun, he was out there in the real world – and here she was by his side, sparkling with excitement as he took her hand and whispered: "One day it'll be you up on that stage. I bet you . . ."

Grace Hari gave a spectacular performance, and by her third encore Jess's hands were sore with clapping. Everything had been so perfect she couldn't believe there were more treats in store. Then Luke said casually, "Come on, quick, or we'll never make it."

"Make it where?" said Jess, bewildered.

"Backstage, of course," said Luke. "I'm going to see if I can get a couple of quotes from her." Jess was speechless. She was actually going to meet Grace Hari!

Somehow, Luke managed to talk his way backstage to the dressing room. Somehow, there was Grace herself, smiling at them. Luke put his arm round Jess and introduced her. "She's a singer too," he announced. Jess was embarrassed.

"Well, not really, only a bit," she blurted out. "Not

16

compared with you. You've been my favourite singer ever since I first heard you on the radio years ago and you did that old Gabrielle number."

"Oh, I still love that," said Grace, obviously pleased. She was quite willing to chat to Jess and answer all her questions about the music she chose and the songs she wrote. She wished her luck in her career as they said goodbye.

"Well done, Jessica Mackenzie, girl reporter," said Luke as they clambered back into the car. "You did all the work for me – and thanks to you I've got some great quotes."

"But I was only asking her what I wanted to know," Jess blushed.

"Exactly," Luke explained. "That's the whole art of interviewing. You just have to make sure that what you want to know is the same as what your readers want to know. You did pretty well."

On the way home Jess chatted happily to Luke, telling him about her first impressions of college, her A levels, her friends.

"It seems such a long time ago that I was doing all that," he said. "I finished A levels last year and then spent a year travelling round Europe which is a lot more fun than doing exams. But then, there weren't any girls like you when I was at school." By now, he'd pulled up outside the house and stopped the car. "You're quite something, Jess," he said softly, turning to look at her. "You're talented, funny and . . ." He reached a hand to her chin and turned her face towards him. "And you've got the sexiest lips I've ever seen." With that, he bent down and kissed her – a long, lingering kiss that sent darts of pleasure shooting through her.

"Am I going to see you again?" he asked gently. She nodded, unsure of what to say. She'd been out with boys before, of course – she'd been kissed by quite a few. But no one had ever made her feel so dizzy with joy and at the same time so uncertain about every move.

"Good. I'll call you – and we'll go out to eat. Anywhere special you'd like to go?" Another surge of panic washed over her. She had no idea what to suggest, since the only restaurants she'd been to were the local Indian ones, and the posh Italian one where Mum and Dad occasionally took the family for birthdays. Somehow neither of those seemed right.

"Don't worry – I've got somewhere in mind that I think you'll like," Luke went on, to her relief. Then he kissed her again, still very gently, his hand reaching under her mass of hair to find her neck. His touch was electric. Jess could feel herself trembling.

"Good night, firebrand," whispered Luke. "See you soon."

That night, as she fell at last into a feverish sleep, Jess began to dream that she was diving from a high rock into a vast lake, and something was telling her that she was about to plunge in far too deep.

Three

When Luke picked her up on the following Wednesday to take her out for dinner she had no idea what to expect. Would it be one of those places with endless courses where you had to know which knives and forks to use? What if there were snails or mussels or anything else that she'd no idea how to eat?

She was even more alarmed when she realized they were going all the way to Birmingham. He led her into a very tiny, very loud cafe, full of people he seemed to know who greeted him across the wails of a live Flamenco guitarist. He told her it was a tapas bar and gave her one of his amused glances when she looked blank.

"A tapas bar," he repeated. "You order lots of little snacks and share them. It's Spanish."

It was impossible to enjoy the food that evening because it was all so strange. Luke took charge of the ordering and seemed to enjoy explaining everything to her. "Let's have some tortilla – it's nice, like cold omelette. And with that, let's see, some mushrooms, a bit of seafood salad . . ." Jess let him get on with it and tried to get used to the idea of dipping into a lot of strange little dishes without having much idea what was in any of them.

She stared round at everyone else. They were all engaged in animated conversations – laughing, waving their bread in the air, toasting each other. She had the distinct feeling that she was the only one who didn't feel at home in this noisy, friendly little restaurant. And yet she wanted desperately to be part of it all – part of this crowd, that was clearly where Luke belonged.

The following Saturday night, Jess lay sobbing uncontrollably, the pile of screwed-up tissues mounting all round her. Next to her on the sofa, Luke was regarding her with a look of puzzled disbelief. On the TV in front of them, Meg Ryan was driving through the night, electrified by the lonely tones of Tom Hanks.

"I'm sorry," Jess burbled through her tears. "I don't know how many times I've seen *Sleepless in Seattle*, but it always gets to me!"

"I just don't believe you sometimes," Luke said affectionately. "One minute you're a fairly normal human being. Then you get up on stage and become a wild Amazon with a voice like a police siren bumping into a cattle truck. And then all of a sudden you're just a little girl who cries at a junky piece of Hollywood nonsense."

"I don't think it's nonsense," protested Jess hotly. "It just happens to be one of my favourite films of all time. And I had hoped it would be romantic watching it with you."

"Ah, well, if romance is what you're after, you've come to the right guy." Luke pulled her lazily towards him and kissed her, his arms tightening round her. "I'll show you romantic – forget Tom Hanks!"

Jess snuggled up to him, still sniffing. There was something very comforting about being in his arms, sinking into his kisses, accompanied by the sentimental screenplay on the TV. She was sorry that Luke didn't share her love of slushy films. It was the first sign of any difference between them. She adored tearjerkers. He liked tough action films. She liked reading romantic novels. He preferred lean American thrillers. But then, she told herself, there was no rule that said you both had to have the same taste in everything. And besides – Luke seemed to find the differences rather endearing.

"There's so much to show you, Jess," he'd say. "There's a whole world out there that I can introduce you to." It was almost as if he looked forward to teaching her the things he knew – as if he relished being more worldly and more experienced.

"I'm not a child, you know," Jess protested, when he'd first said that, earlier that week. "Why are you so keen to treat me like one?"

A shadow passed over Luke's face. "Of course you're not," he said, scowling. "But you're not exactly a woman, either. At least, you're still young enough and sweet enough for me to trust you."

"What do you mean?" demanded Jess, still feeling insulted. Then, suddenly, light dawned. "You're talking about someone else, aren't you? Some other woman?"

"There was someone," Luke admitted, his face creased with bitterness. "She was a woman all right. Imogen. She was gorgeous, sophisticated, knew exactly what she was doing and where she was going . . . And she forgot to tell me I wasn't part of the big life plan."

Jess looked at him expectantly, and after a pause he continued.

"I don't want to talk about it, Jess. Let's just say that I had a few illusions shattered, that's all. Tough can be cruel, strong can be selfish, and a woman who likes to be in charge is really just a woman who likes to grind you under her heel. In Imogen's case her very expensive stiletto heels which can be very painful. Especially when some other guy could afford to buy them for her . . ."

He looked into Jess's eyes and cupped her chin in his hand.

"I'm not going to make that mistake again," he said, kissing her very softly. "You're different, Jess. This time, with you – it's like looking at the world through new eyes, your eyes. And I want to be the one to open them . . ."

Jess wasn't completely satisfied. She resented Luke's assumption that she was so very young and naïve. But at the same time she was flattered that this gorgeous, hunky guy had chosen her. And she was intrigued by him, too – he was so much more experienced than she was, in every way.

"I don't know how you can be so innocent," he was saying now, holding his face close to hers. "So innocent and yet so inviting . . ." Then he was kissing her again, more passionately, pulling her down beside him and taking her in his arms.

Jess's arms had crept round his neck and she felt as though she was melting into his long, passionate kisses. It was as if their lips were welded together so that they were one mouth, one endless embrace. Now they were lying side by side, and Luke's hand moved slowly, expertly down her back, urging her closer to him.

She froze. This was too much, too fast. And it scared her. She wanted to stop him but couldn't think of the words. But Luke had sensed that she had become tense, and gently released his hand.

"Like I said," he murmured. "There's so much I want to

show you. But all in your own time." Then he kissed her tenderly, and casually got up to make some coffee.

It was something she was going to have to get used to, Jess thought. One minute she felt happy and comfortable with Luke. Then suddenly she'd tense up and become tongue-tied and confused. She'd tried to explain it to Ellie, but it was difficult to find the words.

"He's lovely, you know," she began one lunchtime in the canteen.

"But demanding?" suggested Ellie, who was always keen to get down to basics.

"No, not exactly demanding. More like sophisticated."

"Sophisticated!" repeated Ellie. "You mean, he takes you to expensive places."

"No – not exactly. I mean, he acts sophisticated."

"You mean – he doesn't do elephant jokes and he doesn't make his ice-cream into soup before eating and he doesn't do all those boy noises?"

"No, not exactly . . ."

"Oh, for heaven's sake!" Ellie burst out, infuriated. "If you say *no, not exactly* one more time, I'll stop being your friend and I'll tell the whole of our year that you've got every Kylie Minogue single and I'll . . . I'll phone up Luke myself and find out just how supercool he really is!"

"Well, I wouldn't exactly say supercool," answered Jess. Ellie whopped her over the head with her yogurt spoon.

"You really are hopeless, Jess the mess," she taunted. "I'd say you just don't know when to enjoy the moment. You've got this immaculately hunky boyfriend, he's gorgeous, he's clever, he's got a car, he likes you, he doesn't seem to have any obvious vices. So why look for problems? Just accept the fact that he's older than you. You should be flattered."

Jess let it go then. She knew that Ellie was right. She did worry too much. It would be much better to relax and have fun, like Ellie always did. Even now she was launching into the tale of her latest romantic disaster.

"So what do you do when you happen to be seeing two people at the same time and they find out? I mean, it was a piece of incredibly bad luck, really. Or bad timing. But that's what you get for not thinking ahead. I was doing the washing for my mum and I'd asked Oliver to come along and keep me company. The trouble was, I'd forgotten about going to that film with Reece last week."

"Why did that matter?" asked Jess, enjoying the story.

"It probably wouldn't have," reflected Ellie. "Only I accidentally spilt a chocolate milkshake down his T-shirt, so I said I'd wash it and he could come round to collect it. So I did. And he did. My sister let him in and he walked straight into the kitchen where Oliver was making coffee, just as I was taking it out of the dryer. So he recognized it, swiped it off me and buried his face in it, and said he thought it still faintly smelled of my perfume. Oliver just stared at him with his mouth open and he looked really put out and stormed off and now I've got all this explaining to do . . ."

"That'll teach you to get them to do chores with you," giggled Jess.

"No, the moral is I should never have offered to wash the shirt," mused Ellie. "Anyhow, I don't suppose you and Luke have time to do boring things like washing. What've you been up to, anyway? I haven't seen you properly for at least a week, and all you've told me about is that time you went to see Grace Hari, you jammy doughnut."

"Well, we haven't exactly established a routine or anything," Jess said casually. "Last week we went out for a meal." She waited for Ellie's reaction and noticed she looked suitably impressed. "It was quite a nice place, actually – Spanish. We had to drive to Birmingham. Not bad at all . . ."

She just couldn't find a way to tell Ellie how she'd really felt that evening – how awkward and out of her depth. So instead, she decided to impress her.

"It was a tapas bar," she was saying now to Ellie. "You know – you order lots of little snacks and share them. Really delicious. I enjoyed it." Well, she had enjoyed being with Luke and allowing him to help her to all the different dishes, even feeding her the odd forkful of strange salads and spicy sausages.

"It's like going into a different world, being with him," she said dreamily.

"Lucky old you," Ellie said. "So what else is new?"

Jess remembered something Luke had mentioned just the other day. Apparently some of the local Amberley businesses were getting together to fund a Christmas pantomime to raise money for charity.

"They're auditioning next Monday," he'd told her. "And I think you and your friends should go along. The idea is to be a showcase for local talent and they're hoping for lots of young people to take part."

Jess looked at him curiously. "A pantomime? Doesn't sound your sort of thing at all."

"You'd be surprised," retorted Luke. "I happen to be very fond of pantomimes. Besides . . . my paper is one of the sponsors, and they've asked me to be involved in the music. At least," he amended his rather sweeping claim, "the paper's music editor, John Bottrell, is going to direct the music and I'm supposed to help. Anyway, it's going to be fun. I know a few people who are going to be involved and I reckon you stand a good chance of getting a part. It's high time you did more with that voice of yours than let it scream."

Jess was surprised and rather offended. Luke had never

scoffed at what she did before. He'd been impressed when he first heard her singing with the band. She decided to ignore the remark. After all, he genuinely seemed to believe in her and wanted her to do well. Now she mentioned the pantomime to Ellie.

"Oh, right – there's a poster about it on the bulletin board," Ellie said. "It's going to be *Cinderella*, surprise, surprise."

"Well, we might as well go along and check it out," said Jess. "How about the boys? Do you think they'll be interested?"

"Interested in what?" enquired a familiar voice beside her. Thomas and Ben had appeared, and sat down with the hot dogs, crisps and cans of Coke that they called lunch.

"We were thinking about auditioning for the charity pantomime."

"No way," said Ben immediately. "Count me out. Absolutely not. I'm a no-wig, no-tights sort of guy. I'm a drummer, not a clown."

"I'm a clown," volunteered Thomas cheerfully. "And I even quite like tights. Besides, I'll do anything for a break into showbiz. Count me in."

"You just don't know what you'll be missing," Ellie warned Ben. "All those gorgeous girls in the chorus line, just waiting to be swept off their feet." She suddenly looked all eager and excited. "Who knows – maybe I'll strike lucky this time and meet my very own Prince Charming."

Four

The Town Hall theatre was thronging: crowds of young people milled round the auditorium, some slouching in jeans and hoodies, others limbering up in leotards. No one knew what was going on or what would be expected of them.

Ellie had brought her saxophone.

"I'm hopeless at acting, you know I am," she explained to Jess. "I was wondering if they needed a horn section for the band."

Thomas and Jess had worked up a couple of audition pieces each, as they were always being advised to do by their Theatre Studies teacher. All round them people were reciting, practising dancing steps, reading intently.

Eventually a distinguished-looking man with greying hair and a very tanned face appeared on the stage. He was wearing jeans that looked as if someone had ironed them for him, and a well-worn, very expensive, cashmere jumper. He looked familiar – but Jess wasn't sure whether she'd seen him at the supermarket or on television.

"Good evening," he began, in deep, resonant tones. "My name's Michael Wayne and I'm the director of this season's Amberley spectacular." A murmur swept through the theatre. Michael Wayne was an actor – not a household name, exactly, but he was relatively well-known. Jess remembered now where she'd seen him – in a TV sitcom earlier that year. He'd played a businessman who'd been made redundant and become a house-husband instead, and she'd thought he was quite good.

"Now I'm sure you're all wondering how we're going to choose the cast for this production, especially as I believe it's the first time Amberley has attempted such a venture. Well, the various sponsors of the show and the members of the Amberley Council Arts Subcommittee have agreed that this is to be a local event, by and for the community. And they are very keen to involve as many young people as possible . . ."

As he went on to explain how they would be auditioning and what they were looking for, Jess felt a familiar hand on her waist. It was Luke, who'd sidled up next to her.

"Recognize him?" he whispered. She nodded. "He's local," Luke explained. "He and his wife live in Crampton village. She's about to have a baby so he's decided not to take on any touring for the rest of the year. That's why he's agreed to take on the pantomime . . ."

The auditioning seemed to go terribly slowly, and it soon became clear that it would stretch into the following evening as well. Jess began to feel tired. As she sat back sipping water, she noticed that Luke had joined a group of slightly older people who were hanging round near the stage. She recognized one or two of them from the tapas bar. She also recognized a rather glamorous-looking girl with shiny auburn hair glossed into a bob, and immaculate make-up.

It was Georgia Manley, who'd been in the year above her at school. Jess's mother was quite friendly with Georgia's so she'd known her for a long time. And all that time, Georgia had been ahead of her in every way. When Jess took up horse-riding, Georgia owned her own pony. When Jess and her friends were still playing with Barbie dolls, Georgia was getting make-up kits for Christmas. She was the first girl to go on holiday without her parents, the first girl to go out with a college boy – when she was only fifteen.

Jess had never got to know her very well, but she always saw her as impossibly lucky: confident, worldly, and somehow in a different league from the rest of them. They hadn't seen each other since Georgia left school the previous year, but she knew from her mother's regular bulletins that for the past year Georgia had been working at the Rialto, a big hotel on the outskirts of the town.

Georgia must just have said something amusing, because

Luke was roaring with laughter and she was looking very coy and pretty as if she didn't quite understand why. When Georgia was called up on stage it was clear that she'd made a big hit with Michael Wayne, too. He couldn't take his eyes off her.

She'd chosen a monologue from a rather difficult modern play, but followed it with a chirpy little song and dance which Jess thought must be an old Music Hall number. It was funny and well done, and there was no mistaking the enthusiasm in the director's voice when he thanked her. Luke looked appreciative, too, Jess noticed with a pang.

Then he was beside her again. "What are you going to do?" he wanted to know. "I hope you're going to show off that voice properly. I mean, Jess, you know I'm a big fan of new music. But just this once, how about something with a melody?"

"You sound like my dad!" retorted Jess. Then she grinned. "I think you might get a bit of a surprise." And he did. Because when it was her turn to take the stage Jess launched into an old country number, "Love Letters in the Sand", accompanied approvingly by the rather dejected pianist sitting at the edge of the stage.

She was about to go on to her rehearsed speech, from *Romeo and Juliet*, but Michael Wayne stopped her.

"That was nice – very nice," he said. "Look, dear – can you do an American accent? A Southern accent, I mean?"

"Why, I sure ca-an, honey," drawled Jess at once. "Now you have a nice day, y'all, d'you hear me?"

Michael Wayne laughed. "Not bad, not bad, young lady," he said. "I think you've given me an idea. I'll be in touch later."

"Good girl," said Luke, thumping her on the back. "What did I tell you? Melody!"

Jess was beginning to feel like everybody's youngest sister – she'd been called girl, dear and young lady all in the space of five minutes. But somehow she couldn't summon up much indignation. She felt too happy and excited.

Then it was Thomas's turn. He'd obviously made up his mind to play the clown in a big way. He'd chosen "I Wanna Be Like You" from *The Jungle Book,* and sang it with his back to the audience, swaying his hips suggestively and ending with a flourish in which he coquettishly turned his head, looking back over his shoulder and fluttering his eyelashes. He followed that up with a reading from an Enid Blyton book, which he managed to spice up so that even the most innocent escapades of the Famous Five on their Treasure Island sounded rather suggestive. He was a huge hit.

Jess felt fairly sure that she and Thomas had been a success. And there was no doubt at all that Georgia was going to land a cracking part. Apart from them, Jess thought that there were just a handful of really good players: a couple of other very funny boys, a few older people from the amateur dramatic society, and some people from the year above her at college. But there were to be more auditions the following evening, and Ellie was going to try out for the band the next day, too.

"Come on, we need a drink!" urged Thomas, flinging one arm round Jess and the other round Ellie. "It's tough work getting to the top."

Jess's face fell. Luke had offered to drive her home. As far as she was concerned, there was no contest. She thought about inviting him to come out with the rest of the gang, but she was too late. He was making his way towards her now. He nodded to the others, and told Thomas what a brilliant performance he'd given. Then he took Jess firmly by the arm.

"We really must be off," he said briskly. "Good night, stars." And before she knew what was happening he'd steered her out of the theatre and round the corner to where his car was parked. He drove for a few minutes and pulled up outside a row of tall houses which had been turned into flats.

"Time for you to meet some of my friends," he announced. They climbed up to the very top of the house to what was very obviously a shared flat, shared by boys. It wasn't exactly tidy, and as they went past the open kitchen door Jess couldn't help noticing the teetering pile of washing up stacked by the sink.

Luke led her into a cramped living-room. There were mattresses on the floor instead of proper furniture and about eight people were squeezed together, some drinking coffee, others wine. Georgia was there, of course, and she waved cheerily at Jess and Luke.

"Hi," she greeted them warmly. "I really enjoyed your singing tonight, Jessica – I bet you've landed a good part."

"You both have," added someone else from the corner of the room. "Although I'm willing to bet it won't be the best part."

"Oh, no – I think you'll find that's reserved for a real star," added someone else, handing round a bowl of crisps.

"They mean Jasmine Wayne," Luke explained.

"Who?" Jess demanded, puzzled.

"She's Michael Wayne's daughter – from his first marriage. I think she sort of comes as part of the package."

From then on, the conversation was dominated by gossip about the pantomime and who else might be in for favours from the famous director. Everyone started to shout out wild suggestions, from Jess's old headmistress (who scored 99 on the unlikely scale) to Mrs Willoughby, who ran the garden centre and who rather prided herself on her ability to recite the whole of *The Ancient Mariner* off by heart, which she had attempted to do for her audition.

Soon Jess was settled on one of the mattresses, a cup of coffee in her hand and someone's feet poking into her side. She was beginning to get used to the slightly dreamlike feeling that so often accompanied outings with Luke. His friends weren't that much older than she was – two or three years at most. But there seemed to be a world of difference, somehow, between her sheltered life and this bohemian, casual existence they all shared.

How did Georgia manage it? she wondered enviously. She seemed perfectly at home sprawled on a mattress, arguing spiritedly about whether the Rolling Stones were finally too old to cut it. In fact, Georgia was one of those people who always managed to fit in. And the more confident she seemed, the more awkward and out of place Jess felt.

"How are you doing, sunshine?" whispered Luke after a while. "Do you want to go?" She nodded gratefully. It could be a bit of a strain looking relaxed all the time. Wistfully, she thought of Thomas and Ellie and the rest of their friends who'd all headed straight for McDonalds. Life was so much less complicated with them.

Then Luke took her arm and led her out of the room, his friends smiling as they said goodbye. It was great that they accepted her – and great to be seen by them all as his girlfriend. And greatest of all was the moment they arrived home and he took her in his arms.

"You did so well tonight," he murmured. "I was really proud of you – I know you're going to get a good part and do it brilliantly. And we're all going to have such a good time . . ."

Jess wasn't sure quite what he meant by "all" – but as his lips met hers and she began to melt into his kisses, she ceased to care . . .

A few days later, Michael Wayne called another meeting at the theatre – but this time it was by invitation only. Thomas, Ellie and Jess were all invited and tried to look casual as the announcements of the cast list were made. Thomas was to be an Ugly Sister, playing alongside another boy from their college called Cameron. To no one's surprise, Jasmine Wayne was Cinderella, and someone none of them had seen before was Prince Charming. Georgia was chosen to be Buttons.

"Well, she's got the legs for it, hasn't she?" commented Thomas rather meanly. Jess wondered if he was saying that to make her feel better, just in case she didn't land such a good part.

But he needn't have worried. To her amazement, she was given the part of the Fairy Godmother.

"It was your song that gave me the idea," explained Michael Wayne. "I want you to play the part as a Southern Belle – very down home and country. I think it could be hilarious."

There was going to be a chorus line and a small band. Ellie looked pleased when the music director asked if she would play saxophone for them.

"I knew Ben would be sorry," she remarked later. "The band gets a bird's eye view of the chorus."

"Why? You're not going to be a flying orchestra are you?" asked Thomas.

"No, silly. I mean, when the bird's still on the ground – looking up skirts."

"OK – congratulations all of you," the director was saying. "I'm delighted we've got such a strong cast – we're certainly going to show what Amberley is made of. And, most important, I know we're going to give lots of pleasure to lots of people this Christmas. But a word of warning. We haven't much time to get the show together. It's mid-September now, we open the week before Christmas. That's just three months, folks – and I know you're all busy people with work to do, so all our rehearsals have to be in the evenings and at weekends until the final couple of weeks. So I want your commitment, I want lots of hard work, I want you to take it seriously – because you're in showbiz now."

Everyone cheered and laughed excitedly. Even Mrs Willoughby was beaming. She was going to play the Ugly Sisters' mother. Jess felt so happy that she very nearly hugged her. Instead, she turned to hug Luke, who swung her in the air.

"Now the fun is really going to begin," he said. And right then, she couldn't have agreed with him more.

Five

The chips were sizzling dangerously as Jess turned over the sausages and prepared to crack the eggs. A towel was wound round her wet hair and she wore nothing but a huge stripy bathrobe. She'd already had one disaster when chip fat flew on to the white satin shirt she'd been planning to wear that evening. Now it was draped over a chair recovering from her emergency anti-stain operations. She'd decided to take no chances from now on.

She'd promised Mum that she'd feed her brother Harry and his friend Lewis before she went out that evening. "I know you'll be out yourself later, but your dad and I are going to meet in town after work and go to a film. I'd just feel happier if I knew they'd had something decent to eat."

Jess didn't mind, really. Her parents deserved a night out and she quite enjoyed being in charge, even though it wasn't very restful. Every few minutes a tousled head would appear round the kitchen door with another request.

"Are you sure you're making enough chips?"

"Can we borrow your dvd – the Johnny Depp one? Where do you keep it – under your pillow?"

"Quick! Lewis has hurt himself! He's bleeding to death!"

Actually that had been a bit of a panic. Lewis had been showing Harry how to use all the attachments to his Swiss Army knife and his finger had somehow slipped on the gadget for taking stones out of horses' hooves. A deep gash between his thumb and forefinger was spurting blood and he looked very pale as he trailed after Harry into the kitchen.

Jess had taken action immediately, vaguely remembering a First Aid course she'd done at school. She'd grabbed a clean tea towel, folded it into a thick pad, and pressed it hard on the wound. After a minute or so she'd told Lewis to carry on pressing hard.

"It'll stop the bleeding eventually," she told him. "Now, why don't you sit quietly in the living-room and watch your dvd for a bit. Try and hold your arm up, that'll help to stop the bleeding as well."

She'd felt a little less calm when she returned to the kitchen to find the chips sizzling so furiously that they were sending out sparks of burning oil, which was when her beautiful new shirt got spattered. She'd dabbed the spots carefully with stain remover, left it to dry, rushed upstairs for the bathrobe, then rushed down again to check on Lewis's cut hand.

"I don't know," she muttered as she carefully dressed it and put on a plaster. "No one would think that tonight I was going on a dream date to a posh dinner party. I should be bathing in asses' milk, not tending to the needs of two teenage toddlers."

"Oh, not Luke the Fluke again," teased Harry. He'd taken to calling Luke this ever since Luke had caught him out with a very complicated card trick.

"Don't call him that!" said Jess automatically.

"OK, how about your Trump Card?" suggested Harry.

"Or the Joker," added Lewis helpfully, beginning to cheer up.

"What d'you think you'll get to eat at the posh dinner party then?" enquired Harry. "Caviar? Oysters? Lobster?" he mused, rapidly running out of exotic foods.

"Well definitely not sausage, egg and chips," Jess told them briskly. "Which reminds me . . ."

Secretly Jess had been wondering exactly the same thing. She was hoping desperately that she wouldn't be confronted with anything too unfamiliar. She still hadn't quite recovered from the tapas bar. But what did people give you to eat when they invited you for dinner? Her experience was rather limited. She and Ellie had occasionally cooked up spaghetti bolognese for the gang, followed by mountains of chocolate ice-cream. And when her mum had friends over, it was usually for something really simple like casserole – or turkey, of course, for Christmas.

Jess sighed as she scooped out the chips and piled them on to plates for the boys. It was so exciting to be going round with Luke, meeting his friends, being accepted as part of the gang. But there was a kind of anxiety about it all, too. This evening, for example, they'd be visiting Leah and Alex, who were both students at Wolverhampton University and lived together in a little flat in town. It all sounded incredibly glamorous to Jess. She wondered if she and Luke would ever get to the stage where they'd be living together, in a little flat, with their own sofa and a fridge full of posh cheeses and beer and loads of spices to cook with . . .

She was just putting the tomato ketchup on the table and saying, "Here you are, the main course with a bit of food on the side," when the doorbell rang. Harry rushed to answer it.

"It's the King of Hearts," he chortled, very pleased with himself.

Jess squawked. "What are you doing here? You're much too early."

"Oh, they let me go early because I'd achieved the work of six men already," Luke explained airily. "I knew you'd be pleased." Unperturbed, Luke strode into the kitchen. As usual,

Jess's heart gave a little flip when he peered round the door. He was such a stunning-looking guy. Her stunning-looking guy.

He looked her up and down, from her wet hair down to the stripy bathrobe and on down to the old trainers with the holes in the toes.

"Why, Miss Mackenzie," he said, putting on an American accent. "I never realized. You're so gorgeous without your clothes on."

Jess tried to look casual. "Tell you what, boys," she said at once, "why don't you take your supper into the living-room and carry on with your dvd?"

As soon as they'd left, Luke took her in his arms and ran his hands down her back.

"Mmm . . ." he murmured. "I like what you're wearing under this flattering robe." Then he kissed her and Jess felt the familiar, melting sensation as they stood locked together in a long embrace. Then he gently held the lapels of the bathrobe, and for a moment she panicked that he might pull them apart. But he didn't. He just looked deep into her eyes.

"You don't know how gorgeous you are, do you, Jess?" he said quietly. And then he quickly pushed her away. "Go on, you'd better start getting ready. We'll have to leave in an hour. I know – I'll help you dry your hair."

Luke carefully dried and brushed her hair, a strand a time, while she sat at the kitchen table doing her make-up and feeling blissfully happy. It felt so comfortable when they were alone like this. Luke managed to make simple things like hairdrying and doing make-up seem even more intimate than kissing. She wondered if this was what living together would be like? Perhaps she'd be able to tell by watching Leah and Alex.

She was relieved when dinner turned out to be spaghetti. It made her feel at home – even though the sauce was a little spicier than anything she and Ellie had ever attempted, and even though it was served with real Parmesan cheese you had to grate yourself, and a salad full of different kinds of lettuce with a very tangy dressing; even though they were eating off a bare, gnarled wooden table with candles in bottles which flickered excitingly and made everyone look dark and mysterious. Leah was very friendly and asked her all about her A level course and the pantomime. She was studying English and really seemed interested in what Jess was telling her.

"I don't know," she said, "it doesn't seem any time since I was at Sixth Form College, but you seem to be having much more fun than we did. I'd have loved the chance to do all that acting. I suppose you must be in the final year, too. How do you find the time?"

"Oh, no – I've only just started," Jess explained. "I joined the college last month."

Alex laughed. "You dirty old cradle snatcher!" he teased

44

Luke. Jess felt awful – embarrassed and angry at the same time. But Luke didn't seem at all put out.

"Oh, she's mature for her age," he said casually. "And she's a quick learner." Everyone laughed, then Leah poured some more red wine and started asking Jess about which Shakespeare plays she'd be studying. Soon Jess was deep into a discussion of *Antony and Cleopatra* and enjoying herself far more than she'd imagined possible.

After the main course there was fresh fruit and chocolate. Then someone suggested a game of Scrabble.

"Tell you what, Jess," suggested Alex. "Since we did all the hard work preparing dinner, why don't you go and make the coffee."

Jess felt rather like a condemned woman as she made her way into the kitchen. Her heart sank when she saw a glass jug and coffee machine on the cluttered worktop. Next to it was a packet of coffee beans. Coffee beans! She'd never made real coffee in her life and had no idea how to go about it. She remembered Alex's quizzical smile as he'd spoken to her and felt sure it was all part of some awful test to see if she was good enough for Luke.

For what seemed like several hours, but was probably a couple of minutes, Jess stood motionless in the kitchen, completely at a loss. She was just wondering if there was any instant coffee anywhere, when Luke appeared in the doorway.

"I thought as much," he said triumphantly. "It's mean of Alex to have put you on the spot like this. Look, let's make the coffee together."

He showed her how to grind the beans by standing behind her and guiding her hands. Then he walked her over to the jug, still close behind her, and together they prepared the coffee, touching all the time. While it was brewing, he turned her to face him.

"You really are an ingénue," he whispered, brushing her lips with his.

Jess knew he meant she was naïve and innocent. She'd come across the term at college. But she played along with him.

"A what?" she asked, opening her eyes wide. "Did you say genius? Thanks very much."

"Sometimes I just think you're a witch," he said. And then, once again, she was in his arms and they were kissing so hard that nothing and no one else existed in the whole world.

"As long as you can make this kind of magic, who cares if you're hopeless in the kitchen?" he whispered fondly.

"That's not fair," retorted Jess. "Just because I haven't made coffee before doesn't make me hopeless." She remembered how Luke had walked in on her earlier that evening, dishing up supper. "I can do a mean egg and chips, and my sausages are unbeatable." But Luke just laughed fondly. Jess got the feeling he enjoyed thinking of her as helpless and impractical. And somehow, the more he liked it, the more incompetent she seemed to get.

"Look, I'll go back to the others and you bring in the coffee as if you've done it all yourself," he suggested. Jess was sure that no one would be fooled for a minute, but she agreed and busied herself putting cups and saucers on a tray.

No one took much notice of her when she slipped back into the living-room. They were setting out the Scrabble and arguing over who would keep score. Jess carefully began pouring the coffee and handing it round. As she passed a cup to Alex, Luke looked up and said indulgently: "See how well she's doing!"

At that moment Jess's hand jerked involuntarily and the cup went shooting out of her hand. Coffee scattered everywhere and the cup smashed. Somehow, a jagged piece flew into her hand and blood began to spurt from a deep cut.

"Oh, dear – you poor thing," said Leah at once, fussing over her.

"I'm OK," muttered Jess, overcome with embarrassment. "I – I just don't know what happened. I'm really sorry about the cup."

"Don't worry," Leah reassured her. "We've got loads. Look, I'll mop up and Luke, you see to Jess. What a nasty cut!"

Jess could hardly believe what was happening. Just a couple

of hours ago she'd been briskly and calmly mopping up Lewis's wounded hand and dishing out supper. Now here she was again only this time, she was the clumsy one with the cut hand. And Luke was treating her as if she was Lewis's age, only younger.

"It's OK, don't worry," soothed Luke, carefully dabbing at the cut with a length of toilet paper.

"Look, I just need a cloth to press on it and I'll be fine," Jess tried to say. But no one was taking any notice. So she tried again. "Just leave me alone and I'll be fine!" she shouted. Leah looked sympathetic. Alex looked amused. Luke put his arm round her.

"My little firebrand," he said affectionately. "I think perhaps we should go."

As he was driving her home he glanced at her curiously. "You seem a bit upset, sweetheart. Is it your hand?"

Jess took a deep breath. "No. It's not that. It's just that I wish you wouldn't treat me like a kid sister or something. I'm not totally helpless, you know."

Luke looked astonished. "Of course you're not. You're a terrific singer. And an OK guitarist." He paused and grinned. "And a world-class kisser. It's just that you can be a little bit clumsy, darling, where practical matters are concerned. Don't worry, it's not so terrible. In fact, I think it's very sweet indeed."

"I do wish you'd stop calling me sweet all the time," Jess retaliated crossly. "Sometimes I think you want to make out that I'm hopeless just to make you look good. What's your problem – didn't you have any sisters?"

"As a matter of fact, no I didn't," replied Luke lazily, refusing to get offended. "But this has nothing to do with gender, you know. My mother happens to be a DIY genius, so maybe I get it from her. I can't help it if I'm more practical than you are. When it comes to some things, I'm completely helpless."

Once again, the evening ended with a kiss that sent Jess's senses reeling, leaving her with her usual mixture of delirious happiness and obscure anxiety. She lay awake for ages that evening, wishing she was in Luke's arms. And wishing that the two of them were the last people left on earth.

Six

Jess stood on stage, her hands on her hips, staring in genuine wonder at the pouting girl facing her. Jasmine Wayne was someone who was used to getting her own way and it wasn't going down very well.

"I just think this whole lizard and mouse thing is so corny," she whined. "Couldn't we . . . like . . . do a new spin on the story? I mean it is a pantomime, isn't it? How about we get a lot of homeless people and give them jobs as coachmen and things? Or I know – we've got a whole lot of travellers squatting in the garden and I have to go and turn them into servants!"

"Can you believe this kid?" Georgia whispered to Jess. "I mean, talk about spoilt! If we're not careful we'll have Prince Charming agreeing to fund a helpline for people Cinderella doesn't like the look of!"

Jess couldn't help agreeing with Georgia. Jasmine was

outrageously spoilt and her suggestions were insulting as well as absurd. But she felt a little awkward when Georgia badmouthed her. Jess wondered if it was because she could so easily imagine Georgia saying awful things about her, too.

"She goes to that posh girls' school in Birmingham," Georgia went on. "So she probably thinks she's doing us all a big favour slumming it in the sticks."

Michael Wayne sighed in a long-suffering sort of way. He treated Jasmine much more like a difficult starlet than like his own teenage daughter. Jess supposed that was because he'd split up from his first wife years before, when Jasmine was only eight, and he only saw her occasionally.

"It's a pantomime, luvvie," he explained wearily. "A traditional form of Christmas entertainment. People want lizards and mice and coachmen and pretty frocks. It's the way it is. Now just try the scene again – with a little bit of pathos this time, OK, honeybunch?"

He had drawn up a strict timetable for rehearsals. You only had to show up for your own scenes for the first month and for Jess that meant Tuesday and Thursday evenings – along with Thomas and his Ugly Sister and Georgia, who was Buttons. And Cinderella, of course. Michael called them his Kitchen Cabinet because so many of their scenes together took place in the kitchen.

Jess's mum, who was terribly proud of her, was also

51

worried that the pantomime might get in the way of her studies. So she'd made a firm rule, which Jess had had to agree to, that she must be in by eleven o'clock during the week. Otherwise, no pantomime. They were only into the second week and already Jess was finding her curfew a terrible restriction.

"It's even worse than Cinderella's," she complained. "Couldn't you make it midnight – it's more traditional." But her mother just laughed and shook her head.

"I'm sorry, Jess, but Cinderella didn't have A levels to think about. And maybe if she had she wouldn't have had to count on meeting a rich man to take care of her."

But that was no comfort to Jess, who knew she was missing out on all the fun the others had after rehearsals. Even now, while she was busy trying to turn Cinderella into a beautiful princess, she could see Georgia and Luke sitting in the stalls, having a really good laugh about something. "Probably me," she told herself gloomily, trying for the umpteenth time to wave her magic wand.

"Michael, does it *have* to be a magic wand?" she asked suddenly, trying not to sound like Jasmine. "I mean, I am supposed to be a country Fairy Godmother. How about a whip?"

"Brilliant!" Michael snapped his fingers excitedly. He loved what he called flashes of inspiration. Now he turned to Luke and John Bottrell. "Could we have a sort of hoedown riff and a crack of the whip when she first appears? Then every time she transforms something, there's another crack of the whip?"

"That is just so unfair!" complained Jasmine, as Luke and John began to confer. "How come country and western Fairy Godmothers with whips are allowed if we're supposed to be so traditional?"

"Now, now dear," intervened Mrs Willoughby unexpectedly. "What you need to know about the theatre is the director knows best. It may just be that some ideas are better than others." She sniffed disapprovingly. "And I for one certainly could never have supported a production which was uncharitable enough to mock the poor, particularly at Christmas."

"So I'm stuck with lizards and mice," muttered Jasmine, obviously unable to know when she'd lost. Michael, however, was staring at her with a gleam in his eye.

"You're giving me a great idea!" he declared. Everyone else looked apprehensive. Michael seemed to have so many sudden ideas, most of which entailed changes to the script or the music if not the whole storyline.

"I want you to try being a modern Cinderella," he said, thinking aloud. "You behave like any teenager who's grounded, then the Fairy Godmother appears and you think she's gross, and you refuse to collect all those lizards and rats and things because you don't touch slimy creatures and nothing's going to make you." Jasmine looked even sulkier, and drew in her breath as if she was about to speak. But he stopped her.

"Perfect! I want you to look exactly like that! Curl your lips even more, that's right, and give a kind of shudder every time there's a mention of reptiles."

"Well, maybe he does know how to manage that brat of his after all," Georgia shrugged at the end of the rehearsal. "Coming out for a coffee, Jess?"

Jess shook her head regretfully. "I can't. I've got to get home."

And even though Luke took her arm and led her away, even though he drove her home and kissed her as sweetly and as passionately as ever, Jess couldn't help feeling miserable. As he drove off she was sure he was making straight for the all night coffee bar to meet Georgia and the others. And who knew where he got to all the other weekday nights when she was stuck at home studying? She'd never liked to ask him directly, but she was sure that he was out clubbing, at least sometimes. And it was a world where she just didn't belong . . .

She adored the pantomime, though – and at the very next rehearsal she realized just what an opportunity Michael had given her. Luke and John had worked out a wonderful fast country hoedown for the band to play as she appeared, cracking her magic whip. And to announce the fact that she was the Fairy Godmother they'd written a song for her which was the theme tune of the whole show. The chorus went:

It's the magic – the magic of love
A love that has to be true
And if you – if you truly believe
Then one day it will happen to you.

Jess was to sing it as a solo when she first appeared; then as a duet with Georgia, as Buttons, to cheer him up after Cinders has gone to the ball. And then finally with the whole cast at the end when she'd transformed Cinderella into a princess for the last time. She loved the hammy country style that Michael had suggested, and it suited the song perfectly.

As well as that, though, Michael had invented an entirely new comic sequence involving Cinderella's revulsion at the idea of all the reptiles. He'd decided to create a couple of giant rats who would try to get the audience to help them escape. Since Cinderella was refusing to have anything to do with them, it was up to the Fairy Godmother to catch them.

"Oh, but we're not gonna get caught, are we?" they'd say to the children, leading up to a traditional: "Oh, yes you are/Oh, no we're not!" exchange. Finally, they'd creep up behind Jess, who would be asking the children if they'd seen those wretched rats anywhere. With any luck, they'd have a lot of roars of: "They're behind you!" and Jess would have to keep turning round and losing them. She was thrilled – she'd never thought she'd get to play real pantomime slapstick.

"But darling, what's Cinderella without the transformation scene?" Michael pointed out. He explained that most of the money supplied by the sponsors would be spent on costumes and special effects. The most important costume, of course, was Cinderella's ballgown. The most important effects were the Fairy Godmother's magic, which turned the heroine from a ragged scullery maid into a ravishing princess.

Jess worked harder than she'd ever worked at the rehearsal that evening. Out of nowhere, it seemed, Michael had produced two rats, a couple of boys called Matthew and Graham who Jess recognized from college. Michael really knew a lot about stagecraft and spent ages teaching the three of them how to move and work together to create the best comic suspense. By the end of the evening they were all hoarse with laughter. "How am I going to keep a straight face when we do the real thing?" Jess wanted to know, still giggling.

"You'll be amazed," Michael told her. "Once they're in their costumes they won't be these two clowns any more, they'll be rats. Trick number one: you won't be able to see their faces. Trick number two: if you do your bit properly you won't see them at all until the end of the routine."

Exhausted, Jess went to find Luke, who'd long since finished that evening's music session, held in a nearby hall, and was sitting at the back of the theatre, engrossed in a thriller.

"*Dead Man's Footsteps*," she read over his shoulder, making him jump. "Why are you so keen on murder and violence? It's not healthy."

Luke shrugged. He was mad about whodunnits and couldn't understand why Jess found them so off-putting. "You'd enjoy them, you know, once you got into them. This one's really gripping . . ."

"How's the music going?" Jess wanted to know as they left the theatre together.

"Not bad," he said. "We've had to hire a banjo player and steel guitar just for your country number. But I was saying to Georgie that maybe we should play down the country style for your duet."

A dart of anxiety shot through Jess. "Oh, what was she doing at the band rehearsal?" she asked, trying to sound casual.

"She wanted some extra singing practice because she knew she wouldn't be needed while you were playing with the rats," replied Luke almost too quickly, Jess thought. "She's not a natural singer like you, Jess," he added, as if to make her feel better. "She's sensible enough to know that, so she's decided to come along to band rehearsals whenever she can. Of course, she can't always make it because she has to work late quite a bit."

Jess changed the subject abruptly. She couldn't help being jealous of Georgia and her relaxed, easygoing manner when she was around Luke and his friends. But she knew it was best not to let him know how she felt.

"How's Ellie doing?" she asked. Luke grinned.

"Your mate Ellie is unbelievable," he said. "All that energy! I'm amazed she ever manages to stop talking long enough to put the sax in her mouth, let alone play it. But she's good, when she lays off flirting with the rest of the musicians and puts her mind to it."

Suddenly Jess realized how much she missed talking to Ellie. Of course they saw each other at college quite a bit. But they hadn't had a proper talk for a couple of weeks at least, and they hadn't been out anywhere for ages. Jess had been too bound up with Luke to go anywhere or do anything that didn't involve him. And somehow that always seemed to mean going out as a couple or getting together with his friends.

What she needed, she told herself, was a good long girls' evening where they could have a laugh and a gossip and then get down to some real talking. Maybe Ellie would know why falling in love felt so much like going on the biggest ride at Alton Towers: fast, high, dizzying, frightening – and the most exhilarating, ecstatic adventure in the world.

Seven

Jess and Ellie were slouching in the kitchen, idly waiting for their Pop-Tarts to pop. It was Saturday morning and they'd planned a marathon day out.

"How long do we need for shopping?" wondered Jess. "There's masses I want to look at but I've only got enough for . . ." she counted her money for the sixth time. "Well, maybe one top. And a Big Mac. And some more hair beads. How about you?"

"I need some jeans and a present for my mum," Ellie was saying. Then the doorbell rang and they both stopped talking. They overheard Jess's mother answering the door, and then a very strident voice wafted through the hall.

"Sorry to bother you on a Saturday morning, dear, when you must be so busy. But I was just dropping by to see about the raffle tickets for the Charity barn dance next week. You did promise to take a few off my hands . . ."

"It's Mrs Manley!" Jess hissed. "Stuck-up Georgia's even more stuck-up mother."

"I don't think Georgia's all that stuck-up really," whispered Ellie reasonably. "Is she your mum's friend?"

"Well, they know each other," Jess replied. "But I wouldn't say they're friends exactly. It's just that she's always getting involved in these charity events and sitting on committees and things and that means she needs all the suckers she can get her hands on to help her with the dirty work." Footsteps, and the strident voice, grew louder.

"I don't mean my mum's a sucker," Jess corrected herself. "But she's got a problem with saying no. Just wait and see."

Mrs Mackenzie, looking harassed but wearing a brave smile, showed her visitor into the kitchen. She was wearing a pair of jeans and a T-shirt with a big slogan on it proclaiming: DULL WOMEN HAVE IMMACULATE HOUSES. Mrs Manley looked immaculate, in a crisp beige suit and high heels, even though it was nine o'clock on Saturday morning.

"Hello, girls!" she greeted them with a gushing smile. "How are you? My Georgia's been telling me all about you and how hard you're all working on the pantomime." She turned to Jess's mum. "So good for them to have something focused to do in their spare time, isn't it? I do think it's marvellous of Michael Wayne to take on such a worthwhile project. I mean, they are only amateurs, it's not as if it's going to bring him any glory, is it?" Then she simpered a little. "Although of course little Georgie is rather exceptionally talented. And naturally your Jess is a very nice singer . . ."

Ellie kicked Jess under the kitchen table. Jess got the hint at once.

"Er . . . well, we really must be going," she muttered. "So much to do . . ."

"Just like my Georgia, always in a rush," commented Mrs Manley. "Mind you, of course it's very different for her now with this job she's got. She's so busy there, I don't know how they ever managed without her. Just think, she's only been there a year but they're talking about promotion, you know. And the hours she has to work! She's late home most evenings. And then there's the night shift. She has to leave home at eleven o'clock some nights, and she even goes off to work after her rehearsals. I don't know how she does it, I really don't. Bye dears," she added as the girls got up to leave.

Jess's mother grinned at them but didn't say anything. She didn't have a chance. Mrs Manley was in full flow.

"So you'll get rid of as many tickets as you can for me, won't you, dear, and bring the leftovers to the dance. You are coming, aren't you? Oh, and by the way, we're doing a little Harvest Festival Fair for the Senior Citizens next month . . ."

"What a monster!" fumed Ellie, as soon as they were out of the house.

"It's amazing, isn't it?" mused Jess. "That someone so horrible could be involved in so many good works. I wonder why she does it?"

"Boredom," said Ellie at once. "She obviously doesn't have enough to do so she's picked on charity work to get rid of all that energy. Imagine having to be grateful to her!"

"S'pose so," answered Jess. "Anyway, imagine having her for a mother!"

"Wow, yes," agreed Ellie. "The way she was bragging you'd think that hotel couldn't run without her precious daughter. Anyway, she was talking rubbish."

Jess felt a dart of anxiety. "What do you mean?"

"Oh, you know – saying Georgia had to do all that overtime. I mean, she's always hanging around after rehearsals and going for coffee with the gang. She comes to band rehearsals sometimes and never seems in that much of a hurry. So I reckon her mother must be kidding herself. She certainly wants to believe her darling daughter is queen bee."

"No wonder Georgia's so full of herself," said Jess.

"I wouldn't say that, really," said Ellie. "I think you're a bit hard on her, you know, Jess. She always seems to want to be friendly with you."

They'd reached the bus stop by now, so Ellie turned and looked hard at her friend.

"You're not jealous, are you? Just cos she gets on with Luke?"

Jess blushed at once. "Course not," she replied quickly. "Well – not exactly jealous, anyway . . ." she added, not quite able to lie so glibly to her best friend. She was glad when the bus came and Ellie was immediately distracted by the sight of three boys from the year above them at college, all sitting together at the back and waving at them. So for the rest of the journey they sat and chatted with the boys which, as Ellie remarked later, was a very good start to the day.

It was always fun shopping with Ellie, and Jess realized how long it had been since they'd had one of their marathon outings. First of all they tried on hats – lots of hats. Jess was very tempted by a red beret but Ellie thought she looked much better in a black velvet boater with a huge brim and a feather at the back. They very nearly bought a couple of wigs after trying every one in the shop, and then moved on to swimwear.

"Such gorgeous colours," sighed Jess, wriggling out of a red, purple and yellow swimsuit. "Pity we don't have a pool to go with it."

By lunchtime they were exhausted, and flopped down at McDonalds, their arms full of parcels. Ellie had bought a pair of black jeans and a jacket which, she pointed out defensively, was such a bargain that she was actually saving money. And she'd used a similar argument on Jess, who'd fallen in love with a black and white skirt which sparkled with beading and sequins.

"You should get it now," she reasoned. "There's the whole winter ahead of us, so if you buy that skirt it'll save you getting any other party things. Provided you buy a couple of different tops to go with it . . ."

After they'd been happily munching their hamburgers for a few minutes, Ellie began to tell Jess about her latest boyfriend fiasco.

"It's Max – the guitarist in the band. You must have seen him!"

"Of course I have," said Jess. "He looks nice." Not as nice as Luke, of course. But Luke was good-looking in a quiet sort of way. "What's the problem?"

Ellie sighed. "I think I've frightened him off. You see, he's really quiet. And he works in the music shop in town, so he doesn't know the same gang as me, really, and for some reason when he sees me being friendly with people he kind of gets the wrong idea."

Jess couldn't help laughing. "You mean the right idea, surely."

"I don't think that's very nice," retorted Ellie. "I can't help being sociable, can I? He should be able to tell the difference between good honest flirting and – and . . ."

"Good dishonest flirting?" suggested Jess. Ellie giggled good-humouredly, but Jess could tell she was worried.

"I went out with him once and it was lovely," she explained. "We really got on well, and I thought he liked me. In fact, I still think he likes me. But he hasn't asked me out again and I've decided it must be because he thinks I've got all these other boyfriends, even though I haven't."

"Why don't you ask *him* out?" suggested Jess.

"I've thought about that," Ellie told her. "But I'm worried that might frighten him even more. I think I'm going to have to tread very carefully. I mean, he even goes all quiet and sulky when I mess around with your Luke. And quite frankly, Jess, the whole world chats up Luke all the time and you don't mind, do you?"

Jess went quiet. Of course she knew Luke was very popular. She'd seen him laughing and flirting often enough. But she couldn't help feeling a pang when her best friend pointed it out to her.

"Well, not really," she conceded. "I know what he's like. And most of the time it's fine. But just sometimes it really gets to me . . ."

"You don't know how lucky you are," Ellie said. "You've got this gorgeous bloke who's crazy about you. You should be flattered that everyone fancies him and you're the one he's chosen."

"Oh, I know. I am!" Jess assured her. "I've nothing to complain about. He's great – we're really happy . . ." She longed to pour out her heart to Ellie – to try and untangle the mess of emotions whirling round her heart. How could she explain the sneaking anxiety, the moments of panic and insecurity that seemed to go hand in hand with the excitement and joy of being with Luke?

"Maybe it's just the way I am," she said lamely. "I guess I sometimes feel a bit out of my depth. It doesn't matter to him that he's so much older than me – but I think it matters to his friends. They make me feel so . . ."

"You worry too much," Ellie told her, as usual. "Believe me, Jess, the more you fret, the more you drive them away. My advice is just to enjoy Luke. Have fun. Don't go looking for tragedies. And maybe you shouldn't spend every single moment with him, either. Sure, he probably goes out without you sometimes, but that's only healthy. You should do the same."

"Well I am, aren't I?" reasoned Jess. "We're all going bowling tonight, aren't we?"

"Hmm – but that's only because Luke's working. I bet you'd never have come out with us if you could have had him."

Jess knew that Ellie was right, and she felt ashamed. She didn't believe you should neglect your friends when you started going out with someone. But she couldn't deny that was what she'd been doing.

"You're right," she said, slurping down her milkshake. "I've got far too obsessed with him. And I'm really looking forward to tonight. I know, let's go swimming this afternoon so that we're really fit and ready to take on the boys!"

As they marched out of the shopping centre arm in arm, loaded down with carrier bags, Jess felt much happier. It was great being with friends, she decided. Maybe a night out with the gang was just what she needed, to help her make sense of the madness of being in love with Luke Meade.

Eight

It was Jess's turn to bowl and she was bounding with confidence. She stood poised and calm, gently testing the weight of the speckled ball. It was about right. She narrowed her eyes at the pins and took aim. Then rolled. The ball flew down the centre of the alley knocking down five, then six, then a seventh skittle.

"Great!" yelled Ellie. "Now just concentrate and you can put us in the lead!"

There were three of them on each side. With Ellie and Jess was a girl called Molly, who had turned up with Ben. He'd been looking rather smug since they'd met up, as if he was dying to show her off but didn't want anyone to think he was making a fuss about actually having a girlfriend for once. She was small and thin, with very short hair and cool glasses with red frames. Jess liked her at once; she smiled a lot, but in a friendly rather than a nervous way.

"I hope you're not going to be too brilliant," she'd said when Ben introduced them. "I'd never been bowling before, only–" she dropped her voice so that only the girls could hear – "Ben took me last night, to show me how to do it so I wouldn't make a fool of myself." They all laughed then, and Jess couldn't help envying her. Why couldn't she just admit when she was hopeless at something, or new to something, like Molly did?

Thomas and Ben had also brought along Matthew, one of the rats in the pantomime, who was in the same science group as Ben. He was a really earnest person who was so thrilled to be invited that all he wanted to do was please them. So it was Matthew who was sent to get more drinks, Matthew who had to organize their bowling lane and get it changed when the computer went down. Privately Jess thought he was a bit wet to keep agreeing to do the dirty work, but she couldn't help liking him. And the more she smiled at him the more anxious he seemed to do things for her.

"Have you met him before?" whispered Molly, as they started marking up their names for the start of the game. Jess noticed that Ben had called himself KING KONG and Molly was MOLLY. Hesitantly, she put down CLEOPATRA for herself, and Matthew immediately decided he was ANTONY. So when it was Thomas's turn he carried on the joke and called himself ASP. Ellie ignored everyone else as usual and decided on MADONNA.

"Yes, I know him a bit," Jess whispered back to Molly. "We're in a pantomime together. Why?"

"Why?" repeated Molly, pushing her glasses way up into her forehead for maximum effect. "Because he fancies you like crazy, that's why. I've never seen anyone make it so obvious."

"Well, I hadn't noticed," Jess replied. "And even if it was true, he'd be wasting his time. I've got a boyfriend already. He's coming to meet me later."

At that moment, Matthew asked anxiously: "Have you chosen a ball yet, Jess? You need to make sure you pick the right weight, you know. Do you want any help?"

"Oh, *please!*" groaned Ellie. "And she says she hasn't noticed!"

Thomas was the first to bowl, for the boys' team. He was on great form, even by his standards, and spent ages posing with the ball, giving his impression of Steve Harmison, and another of Fred Flintstone, before finally sending it straight down the lane in a perfect strike.

"Yess!" yelled the three boys, clenching their fists and thumping each other on the back. Thomas and Matthew did a quick dance routine, as the two rats from the pantomime, until people on the other lanes started staring at them. "They're not with me," Ben started muttering to no one in particular. "This doctor sort of asked me to look after them and he never came back . . ."

By this time Jess had laughed so much she was beginning to hurt. She'd forgotten how good it was just to let yourself have fun without having to worry about anything. She felt so relaxed with the gang – even with poor Matthew, who was watching Molly anxiously. It would be his turn soon, and he clearly hadn't decided whether to try and win for his team or lose to help the girls.

Molly obviously had no such doubts. She picked up the heaviest ball, walked up to the edge of the lane and chucked it with all her might. Five of the pins went down. She repeated the action for her second throw, and knocked down another two.

"Well done," the girls called, and she grinned at them, clearly not that bothered about who was going to win. She sauntered over to Ben and planted a casual kiss on his cheek. "Had a good teacher, you see," she explained, and he tried not to look too pleased in case anyone noticed.

Matthew managed to score exactly the same number as Molly, which Jess thought was very tactful, if he'd done it on purpose. She couldn't quite believe that, though. No one went to the lengths of not winning at bowling, however much they fancied someone.

Now it was her turn, and she'd already floored seven skittles. There were three to go. Again, she held the ball in front of her, trying to measure the distance with her eyes.

She gave a little skip this time as she bowled the ball, aware of several pairs of eyes focusing on her every movement. The ball smashed into the remaining three pins – and they were down!

Now it was the girls' turn to cheer. Matthew was despatched for more Cokes and crisps while Ellie and Ben took their turns. Thomas glanced at the score. "Hmm," he commented. "Looks like the asp is stinging Cleopatra, Madonna is chasing Antony, King Kong has made off with Molly and, let's see now, we're slightly ahead – but that's only the first round. By the end of the evening, you girls should be well and truly slaughtered, proving once again that there are some things you just don't do as well as we do, and why not just admit it?"

"Oh, what have we here," Molly taunted him. "Surely not an old-fashioned sexist man? I thought they were extinct."

"There was a danger of that," added Jess. "So they opened a zoo for a few remaining examples of the species. And they called it . . ."

"Amberley Sixth Form College!" shouted Ellie.

"Oh, so that's where they keep them, is it?" said Molly innocently. "You see I don't know very much about men because I go to Bailey Girls' High and they don't tell us anything. And I didn't know they still had sexists. What are they like?"

"Well," said Jess, scratching her head. "The ones at our college all have to practise these habits that were disappearing from modern male behaviour. Like talking with their mouths full and burping a lot and telling jokes about their mothers."

"And they've all learned how to pretend that there are some things they're better at than girls," added Ellie, pointing at Thomas, who obediently put on a really macho expression, stuck out his hips and said: "Yeah, and we get advanced lessons in how to call girls chicks and babes."

"And be careful if one of them tells you that you've got a beautiful mind," said Ben, slipping his arm round Molly. "Because we're only after one thing, you know."

Everyone was in fits of giggles by now, especially Jess, who was almost speechless with laughter. "And they're doing an experiment with some of the species," she gasped, in between guffaws. "They're teaching them to open doors for girls and offer to buy them drinks."

At that moment, Matthew returned with a teetering tray of Cokes and crisps. "Well, I hope you all wanted salt and vinegar because that's what you're getting. The drinks are on me, guys." He looked puzzled as the other five collapsed with laughter.

"What did I say?" he asked. "I only said I'd buy the drinks. I don't know, you lot must have weird minds."

"Beautiful minds!" shouted the girls, now in hysterics.

They carried on the game in a manic mood. Everyone was relaxed, even Matthew. Jess was having the time of her life, and her high spirits showed in her bowling. On her next turn she scored a strike and was so pleased with herself that she leapt into the air and ended up doing the splits, then she pretended she was stuck, and everyone had to grab a bit of her and hoist her up again.

Towards the end of their third game, it was Jess's go once more. Flushed with success, she lifted the ball and carefully took aim. She was about to roll it straight down the alley when a familiar voice behind her said: "Good – I've made it in time to see you making a strike!"

It was Luke, of course. At the sound of his voice Jess jerked the ball out of her hand and sent it skeetering into the gutter. Her heart began its usual racing, as the pleasure of seeing him mingled with a sudden awkwardness. Just a few moments ago she had felt so relaxed, laughing and joking with the gang. Now Luke had arrived the atmosphere had instantly changed.

"Wow, you've jinxed her!" exclaimed Molly, who'd never met any of them before but was always happy to speak her mind. "She was playing brilliantly till you arrived."

"Nah, you're just saying that," quipped Luke. "Typical – blaming the man for the woman's inadequacies."

"Never mind, mate," said Ben happily. "She's got a

beautiful mind." And they all laughed, except for Luke, who gave him a long, puzzled look, and Jess herself. She suddenly wanted to leave as quickly as possible. Somehow the jokes didn't seem as funny, now that she was seeing them through Luke's eyes.

"Well sorry, gang, we've got to be going," she said brightly. "It was my last go anyway, so it won't make any difference to the score. See you."

Once they were alone in Luke's car, she felt happier. He was telling her all about how he was supposed to have been reviewing a couple of bands that evening, but the night editor had rung him to say he had to go to the scene of a car accident. They hadn't been able to contact another reporter, so Luke was given the story.

"I was a bit worried, I must admit," he was saying. "I didn't know how I'd cope with all the carnage. But once you've got a job to do you just have to get on with it, even though it's not very nice. You just can't allow yourself to get upset."

Jess thought that was quite good advice for her at the moment. Just do your job of being a fun girlfriend, don't get too involved, she told herself. But at the same time, she was thinking what a fascinating person Luke was, so full of ideas and experiences, and with so much to give.

He drove out of town for a couple of miles, eventually turning down a little track into the woods. There, he stopped the car and turned off the lights. "At last, I've got you to myself," he whispered, taking her in his arms. Then his lips found hers, and all the familiar, dizzying sensations coursed through her as she melted into him, wanting the hungry, urgent kisses to go on for ever and ever.

At last he held her gently away from him and looked into her eyes.

"I want you, Jess," he said softly. "You know that, don't you?" She nodded, her pulse racing with excitement and fear, too.

"I care too much to rush you," he carried on. "But one day, when you're ready, I'm going to make love to you."

"Luke, I – I do want to," she stammered. "It's just that . . ."

"I know. I know you're young and it's a big step," he said. "I understand. But Jess, sometimes there's this gulf between us, and I think that it'll only go away once we become real lovers. Do you know what I mean?"

Jess nodded, but didn't trust herself to say anything. Could it be that Luke was right? If they made love, really made love, would all the awkwardness and confusion really disappear? She remembered how his arrival had made her foul up that last throw at the bowling alley. Was his presence so exciting that she couldn't concentrate on anything else? Or was it just because he always made her feel nervous?

She giggled, and he raised an eyebrow. "What?"

"Oh, nothing really," she said. "I was just wondering if my bowling average would improve if we ever slept together." He shook his head wonderingly.

"Mad, totally barmy," he said affectionately. "However did I get mixed up with this crazy teenager?" And he kissed her once again, before they drove home.

Nine

Jess swaggered on to the stage for the eighteenth time that evening and declared, rather wearily: "Cinderella, you *shall* go to the ball!" It wasn't as though she was saying it wrong or anything – although she was well aware that by about take eight she'd lost some of the conviction she'd been trying to bring to the most famous lines in the whole show. But you couldn't really keep up a Meryl Streep level of acting when everyone round you was measuring up the stage for puffs of dry ice, counting in the lighting and practising whipcracks and thunderbolts.

Besides, Jess was preoccupied. It was her birthday this Saturday, October 31, and she was going to have a party. Her mother had already set the ground rules: she and her friends would have to do the catering; no one was allowed in the bedrooms; she supposed they could make Hallowe'en decorations if they had to, but nothing that would stain. And although she didn't mind a little alcohol as well as soft drinks, she definitely meant a little, and that was that.

Jess had happily settled for all the conditions because in return her mum and dad had agreed to stay out of the way until midnight. Ellie and Thomas were taking charge of the food and decorations. Luke had undertaken to provide the music.

"I can't help with the preparations, hon," he'd warned her. "I'd like to obviously, but I'm working all day. I'll be there for the start, though – with the hottest sounds in town."

Jess sighed. She knew Luke worked hard, but she couldn't help minding his attitude sometimes. He enjoyed his job so much he never seemed to regret the time he spent away from her. "Won't you miss me?" she'd asked him once, when he'd had to work on a Sunday. She'd instantly regretted her words. He'd looked at her strangely and then shrugged. "I don't see it that way. Work is work. You are you. In fact, I'm surprised you'd come out with something like that."

Jess had looked hurt so he'd tried to explain. "The reason I was attracted to you in the first place is that you're so full of energy and talent," he said. "You're always doing things – playing in bands, singing, acting . . . You're your own person Jess, and I like that. I like it very much . . ." Then, naturally, he'd pulled her towards him and kissed her doubts away. "So let's enjoy each other – not tie each other down . . ."

Now, as she cracked her whip yet again and began to weave her magic on poor, tattered Cinderella, she made up her mind to be as independent and as carefree as she had been when she first got involved with Luke. And that meant showing him that she was relaxed about him and not the least bit possessive. Which meant, in turn, that she'd better be very careful about who she invited to the party.

"OK, OK – I think we've got it," Michael declared in a rather harassed voice. "Now let's just run through the rest of that kitchen scene. Cinders, over here. Buttons? Where's Buttons got to?"

"I'll go and find her," volunteered Jess. She was fairly sure that Georgia would be lounging around somewhere backstage. After a quick search she found her in one of the dressing rooms, lying on a sofa reading a paperback that Jess recognized: *Dead Man's Footsteps*. It was the book Luke had been raving about not long ago. This was her big moment, Jess told herself. Don't be jealous, don't start inventing problems. Prove what a nice, easygoing person you are.

"Michael wants you for a kitchen rehearsal," she said to Georgia. Then she took a deep breath. This was it. "Oh, and by the way, I'm having a party on Saturday night and I'd like you to come."

Georgia looked pleased – really pleased. "That's great, Jess, I'd love to!" she said at once. "Come on, let's get back to the pouting primadonna on stage. I swear if I had a half pint of lager for every time Cinderella had to repeat her clinch with Prince Charming, I'd be able to open a brewery by now."

Jess laughed. "Maybe you could offer her a four X!"

She was gratified when Georgia burst into raucous giggles, but deep down, even though she didn't want to, she was wondering whether Georgia had accepted the invitation not because of her but because of Luke. Then she told herself sternly to stop torturing herself, and for the rest of the evening she threw herself into hard work.

The following evening Thomas, Ben, Molly and Ellie were sprawled over her bedroom floor making lists. "Lots of French bread and cheese, pickles, crisps, peanuts," Thomas said, writing furiously. "What else do people eat?"

"Sausages," suggested Molly. "I'll do those if you like. I'll put them on cocktail sticks. Actually, I like putting things on cocktail sticks. How about cheese and grapes – or olives and ham?"

"I know, let's do bacon and fruit pastilles on sticks," said Ellie, and everyone started inventing even nastier combinations.

"Black pudding and Turkish Delight!"

"Spam and orange sorbet!"

"Mars bar with spaghetti and catfood!"

That, of course, was Harry, who'd sneaked into the room licking a home-made ice lolly.

Jess groaned. "Who said you could come in?"

He grinned. "No one actually asked me, but I can always tell when I'm needed. I mean, you're going to want someone to do the decor, aren't you?"

"Oh, no!" snapped Jess at once. "I know all about you and fake blood. And I remember the year you beheaded yourself. And the time you made your eyeballs fall out. And I'm warning you now – don't even think about it!"

Harry looked wounded. "I wasn't going to suggest anything remotely like that," he protested. "I was simply offering myself for heavy duty carrying, lifting and pumpkin carving. Oh, and a little light trick-or-treating, naturally."

"You mean, if people don't give you treats you might bite them on the neck at midnight," suggested Thomas, who'd always had a soft spot for Harry.

"Something like that," agreed Harry. "Or I might just keep a list of who's getting off with who and kind of brandish it as I collect all my treats."

"The little brother from hell," muttered Jess as the others started laughing.

"Tell you what," suggested Ellie. "Why don't we do all the shopping on Friday after college, and then go out for a pizza?"

Jess was about to find an excuse to say no. She always saved

Friday evenings for Luke. Then she remembered that he was going to Birmingham that night to see some bands for the paper. He was going to try to write his reviews the next day in between all the other stories that were piled up for the Saturday shift.

"And because it'll be your very last day of being Sweet Sixteen, we'll treat you!" declared Thomas.

"Wow – shopping in the supermarket!" Ben said to Molly. "I told you that if you stuck with me I'd drive you into the fast lane." Jess wanted to hug him. It was obvious that he was still so besotted with Molly that falling in the mud with her after a wild day cleaning drains would have had its attractions. And he was glad to be able to show her off to his friends, too. If only she could feel that carefree about Luke . . .

As she saw them to the front door she heard a loud, unmistakable voice echoing from the kitchen. The door opened.

"I really must be going now, dear," Mrs Manley was saying, or rather booming. "Thanks so much for agreeing to take on the Meals on Wheels for me next week. I don't know what I'd do without you, I really don't. And Georgia's no help at all now, of course. Do you know, she's got to spend all tonight at that hotel, then there's a rehearsal on Thursday, and then on Friday she's got to work all day, come home and then go back again! Working on a Friday night! I suppose they've discovered that they can't do without her, but honestly, I'm sure they're exploiting the poor girl. Oh, hello!" She suddenly noticed the gang loitering in the hallway.

"Hello, dears – all ready for the party? Georgia's told me all about it. You're not actually dressing up though, are you?"

"Oh, no," Jess answered. "It's come as you please." But she couldn't help adding: "Although you can tell Georgia she can be a witch if she wants to," and they all fell about laughing as Mrs Manley said her goodbyes and swept off home.

Thomas, Jess and Molly did most of the shopping. Ben and Ellie pounced on anything that took their fancy and had to be kept in check.

"Well, why can't we have chocolate and hazelnut spread sandwiches?" they'd demand. Or: "Hey, look – economy size packs of toffee popcorn. We need some. It's a bargain!" Eventually they settled on a sensible amount of party food that would be easy to prepare, and piled it into Jess's father's car. He was waiting patiently for them outside the supermarket, an anxious look on his usually placid face.

"What's up, Mr Mackenzie?" asked Thomas. "It's not us, is it?"

"Oh, no – it's not the party I'm worried about. It's the birthday present. As of tomorrow, this car is under threat."

"Yup," beamed Jess. "I'm getting a course of driving lessons – and you'd think they'd be pleased, wouldn't you?"

"I got that for my birthday," put in Ben helpfully. "And you don't have to worry about a thing, Mr Mackenzie. Young people today are very good with mechanical things."

"Yes, that dent hardly shows now, does it?" added Molly, and they all muffled their giggles as Jess's father turned pale.

They spent most of the evening at the pizza restaurant planning the party and gossiping about the guests.

"Did you invite Jasmine?" Thomas wanted to know. Jess nodded.

"I did in the end. I thought it would be mean not to. She'd only hear about it from the others. Practically the whole cast is coming."

"I know," suggested Ellie. "Why don't you tell her it's fancy dress? Then she can turn up as a vampire, we'll be in ordinary clothes, she'll say why did you tell me to wear fancy dress and we can all say: 'What's the problem? You're not *in* fancy dress!'"

"Let's play that old game, Consequences," suggested Thomas suddenly. "Everybody write down a man's name and then pass on your paper to the next person . . ."

Soon they were all engrossed in dreaming up unlikely venues for romance, and even more unlikely opening lines. They rocked with laughter as they took it in turns to read out the final ridiculous outcomes: Madonna and Ben's dad, Brad Pitt and the Queen.

The last one was Jess's. Everyone looked expectantly at her as she began to read aloud. "Count Dracula met Enid Blyton at Jess's birthday party. He said: You *shall* go to the ball. She said: I'm washing my hair tonight. The consequence was: they invented a new pizza topping. And the world said . . ."

"I like a full-blooded man," suggested Molly.

"Everyone had a bite," put in Ben.

"Even Timmy the Dog!" added Ellie.

"She wanted a happy ending but he just wanted to drink her dry," said Thomas quietly.

Jess stared at him, horrified. It was as if he could read her soul, her innermost fears. How could Thomas possibly understand so clearly her worries about Luke?

"Stupid game," she said lightly. "Probably what happened was that she ordered garlic bread, he disintegrated and nobody got a goodnight kiss."

It was nearly eleven o'clock by the time they left the restaurant and it was fairly quiet outside, even though they were in the centre of town.

"I promised you life would be an adventure with me, didn't I?" Ben said to Molly, carrying on his usual joke, which she didn't seem to mind at all. "That's what I love about this town – bright lights, excitement, always on the go. You will tell me if it gets too fast for you, won't you?"

"How could I ever get enough if it?" replied Molly. "I mean, with any luck we might catch the last bus together. It's all so indescribably romantic!"

The others were straggling along the High Street, joking about what a one-horse town Amberley was – and dreaming about the day when they'd all get out. But Jess had gone silent. As they passed the next set of lights she'd noticed a little green Renault, parked up a side street. She knew the car. She'd have recognized it anywhere. It belonged to Georgia. But Mrs Manley had distinctly said that Georgia was working at the hotel all Friday night – and the hotel was miles out of town.

Jess's mind was racing painfully. Just down the road were the offices of the *Amberley Herald*. Could she be meeting Luke there? she wondered wildly. But that was a crazy thought. It was much more likely that she was at the Peacock Disco. Or even at the Belvedere Hotel just on the corner, which ran a Friday night disco. Jess tried to stem the flow of her thoughts. Why should she be jumping to crazy conclusions like this? It was none of her business what Georgia got up to, and her heart certainly had no right to be beating so wildly.

But an insistent little voice inside her kept reminding her that Georgia had lied to her mother and said she was at work, when in fact she was in town. She'd lied before, too – Jess remembered Ellie scoffing at Mrs Manley's claim that her beloved daughter worked so hard, so many evenings. Then, with another pang, she remembered the book Georgia had been so engrossed in at the rehearsal – the book Luke had so raved about.

When they'd said their goodnights and Jess had gone home, she promised herself that she wouldn't allow her suspicions to get in the way of her birthday. She must simply bury all the treacherous thoughts and concentrate on having fun.

After all, she comforted herself as she snuggled into bed, Luke would be with her tomorrow night – no one else. It would be full of her friends, she'd be at the very centre of attention and everything would be perfect.

Ten

Jess woke up ridiculously early the next morning, aware of a bubble of excitement deep inside her. Even though she was now seventeen, Jess got just as thrilled about her birthday as she had when she was seven. She opened her eyes a fraction and gave a squawk. There was a strange shape on the bed. At first she thought it was a giant tarantula. Then she told herself not to be so stupid, it must be the family cat, Harold. On closer inspection she realized it *was* a giant tarantula, but not a real one. This one was made of an old bowler hat, its legs constructed of coat hangers covered in black tights. Attached to it was a long piece of black cord.

Cautiously Jess slid out of bed and tugged at the cord. Nothing happened. It was attached to something heavy – outside her room. She followed the cord to the door, out onto the landing and down to the bottom of the stairs where it was attached to a huge box covered in black paper. She pulled the string that was tied round it, opened the top flaps, and out popped a second tarantula attached to a spring. Pinned to it was a crudely scrawled message: LOOK INSIDE.

Inside was a smaller box, inside that a smaller one. She was down to her tenth box before she finally got to two small white envelopes. The first contained a computer-designed birthday card from Harry, with two tickets for a Slipknot concert tucked inside. The second was heavier. When she ripped it open she found a card from her parents, and a key. It was the key to her father's car. Yippee! That meant that not only was he buying her the promised set of driving lessons, he was also prepared to let her use his beloved Volvo after all!

Suddenly there was a tremendous crash in the kitchen and Harry came rushing out.

"Get back to bed!" he ordered. "You're spoiling everything! You're supposed to be asleep!" So Jess snuggled back into bed, and a few minutes later Harry appeared with a tray of rather soggy toast, a cup of tea, with only a bit slopped in the saucer, and a glass of what looked like orange juice. "Actually it's Buck's Fizz, orange juice and champagne," he explained. "Happy birthday."

And then her parents appeared with their own glasses of Buck's Fizz, and toasted her seventeenth birthday. "This is so great!" she said, quite overcome. "Why are you being so nice to me?"

"Because we're hoping that if we're really, really nice you'll take care of the house tonight," said her mum.

"And that you'll take care of my car when you start driving it," added her dad.

"And that you'll let me come to the party and help out," piped up Harry hopefully. Jess laughed. "Er – yes, yes and yes!" she said. "You can come to the party provided you do the decorations, pass round food and drink, do all the washing-up, don't tell any elephant jokes, don't tell any light bulb jokes and don't tell anyone any stories at all about me as a child."

Harry looked crestfallen. "Just one light bulb joke?" he pleaded. Jess fixed him with a long stare.

"No jokes. No stories. Actually, could you manage not to talk at all?" But Harry had already sped out of the room, shouting:

"Just going to start the pumpkins. I'm going to make them all look like Mr Pratt, our technology teacher."

After that, the day was one long hectic rush. Ellie arrived at about ten o'clock and presented Jess with a huge pair of earrings. One was a silver moon with an owl, the other was a silver star with a cat.

"I thought you'd appreciate something witchy," she explained. "They'll sort of match the ones I'm wearing." She held up a pair of black bat earrings.

The girls spent the morning clearing the living-room, pushing back all the furniture and removing anything that looked as though it might be fragile. Harry was carving out pumpkins and singing along to Radio One.

After lunch, Thomas and Ben arrived. When Jess opened the front door they stood on the porch, waiting.

"Er – the others are just parking," Ben said.

"Others?" asked Jess. Then she saw Molly making her way up the path with Matthew. She looked questioningly at the boys.

"He wanted to come," Ben explained. "And we thought another pair of hands couldn't do any harm . . ."

They all crowded into the kitchen and handed Jess her presents. Ben gave her some removable tattoos, Molly a friendship bracelet, and Matthew a set of juggling balls.

"Oh, that's just what I need!" she exclaimed, and started practising right away, as the others bustled round making sandwiches, cutting up vegetables and arranging glasses.

The only disappointment was Thomas's present. He just handed her a copy of *Sugar* as he pecked her cheek. She tried to cover up how hurt she felt by rushing round maniacally, telling everyone else what to do. But she was surprised at how much she ached inside. After all, it was her seventeenth birthday. He was one of her closest friends. Surely he could have managed more than a tatty old teenage magazine?

It was only later, when everyone except Ellie had gone home to change, that Jess found his real present. Ellie had brought her party things with her so that they could get dressed together. While she was in the bathroom washing her hair, Jess lay on her bed browsing through the magazine. A little package was tucked between the pages. It was beautifully wrapped in shiny silver paper. Intrigued, she opened it. Nestling in a bed of red tissue paper was a little silver brooch in the shape of a guitar. It was so intricately made that each string was moulded in a shiny finish, and tiny jewels sparkled across the body. She gasped. The brooch was exquisite. And expensive. And more than that, it was a very intimate gift. Who better than Thomas knew how she'd slogged to master the lead guitar and how much it meant to her to be a player as well as a singer? It was a true badge of friendship. Somehow, she didn't know why, her eyes filled with tears.

Jess was wearing tight black jeans and a very glamorous black velvet top with long, voluminous sleeves which fell in soft folds from her elbows, but cut so that her shoulders were bare. Carefully, she pinned the brooch to her chest but didn't mention it, and Ellie barely glanced at it. She was too busy helping her to thread silver and black beads into her hair, which looked great with the new earrings.

"Ooh, you look so Goth!" exclaimed Harry. "Wanna borrow any fake blood for your lips?"

"You both look very nice," commented her mum. "Exotic, but nice. I do think girls are so, um, individual these days, don't you, Bill?"

Jess's dad grunted, looking anxious. "You won't let anyone go near my records, will you, love?"

Jess laughed. "No, Dad, I promise no one will filch your Elvis collection. Don't worry – Luke's bringing his iPod, and I've got loads of good CDs. We won't need to plunder your musical antiques."

Finally she managed to bundle her parents out of the door, as Thomas and the others arrived. They all stood in the middle of the living-room, surveying their work. Harry's pumpkins were arrayed in a row along the windowsill, lit by candles. There were masks, bats and spiders hanging from the ceiling and Harry and Thomas had managed to set up a flickering light show against one wall.

"Oh, it's lovely!" Molly said approvingly. "Very *Homes and Gardens*. Why don't you persuade your mum to keep it like this?"

Ben put on some dance music. "I declare this party officially open!" he said, and to Jess's amazement he grabbed Molly and actually started dancing with her. Jess hadn't even known he could dance. Up until now he'd always refused on principle. Thomas grabbed Ellie and started jiving with her – a routine they'd been practising for hours. That left Jess and Matthew.

He gave her a shy grin, then took her hands and began to dance. He was surprisingly good. Jess found herself being led round the floor, half jiving, half disco-dancing, one minute being pulled into his arms and the next being flung in a spin round the room. As the track finished he steered her towards him, threw her to one side, then the other, and ended with both arms round her waist.

Flushed with the exertion of the dance as well as the general excitement, Jess wasn't sure what to say to him. But at that moment the bell rang, someone flung open the door, there was the sound of chattering and laughing . . . the party had begun.

For the first half-hour or so Jess was so busy greeting her friends, making sure people were offered drinks and had someone to talk to, that she couldn't think at all. Then she started to wonder about Luke. He'd promised to be there by eight and now it was eight-thirty. Where could he be? Surely he'd come soon on this of all days?

She tried to fling herself into the mood of the party, chatting and laughing, darting from group to group, her eyes glittering dangerously, her cheeks flushed. The more she tried not to worry about Luke, the more wildly she'd joke and tease, giggle and show off.

Everyone else seemed to be having a great time. Ben and

Molly were gazing into each other's eyes all the time and feeding each other peanuts. Thomas seemed to be flirting with four girls from college all at the same time. Ellie's face was a mask of ecstasy. Her elusive guitarist, Max, had finally shown up and she was doing everything she could to show him she cared.

Someone found her dad's Beatles collection and put it on for fun. Immediately she and Thomas grabbed Ellie, who'd already grabbed Max, and they began a dazzling impromptu display of rock and roll dancing. The four of them finished up collapsed in a heap on the floor, while everyone else clapped and whistled. Then the next track came on. It was her absolute favourite, the song she'd sung at the talent night when she'd first met Luke: "You Really Got a Hold on Me."

Ben and Molly were locked in a dance that was more of an embrace. Ellie was wrapped round Max. Almost before she'd realized it, Jess found she was dancing again, this time with Matthew. He'd taken her in his arms and was holding her close. He really was a good dancer. Even as her thoughts strayed to Luke and the anxious knot tugged inside her, she was aware of Matthew's strong body guiding her round the floor, aware of his breath very close to her neck.

"You're amazing, Jess," he whispered. "I wish you'd let me get close to you." Jess was about to retort that she had a boyfriend already. That Matthew must be crazy to think she'd go out with anyone else when she had the greatest-looking, most interesting, most fabulous guy anyone could ever want. That he actually had a cheek coming on to her when he'd seen her with Luke, her Luke.

Then she glanced at the clock over the mantelpiece. It was nine-thirty! A flash of panic struck her, quickly followed by something quite new. Anger. It was like a white flame, burning yet cold at the same time. It was her birthday party – and her own boyfriend hadn't even bothered to turn up! How could he treat her like this?

She turned to Matthew and looked him in the eyes. He was good-looking in a mild, unthreatening sort of way. A soft lock of hair fell boyishly into his eyes and strong white teeth protruded slightly from full, sensitive lips. Not exactly sexy, she thought, but he's OK. He likes me. He's a great dancer. And he's here.

Jess didn't say anything but she allowed him to lead her into the kitchen for a drink, and then, quite naturally, out of the back door into the garden. He took her hand as they made their way down the little path to her dad's vegetable patch.

She was glad that Matthew didn't seem to want to talk. Anything they said would have been confusing. But she liked the feeling of his strong hand holding hers, and the look of longing in his eyes as, very tentatively, very slowly, he bent his head to hers in a long, gentle kiss. Jess closed her eyes, feeling him trembling as their mouths touched and melded together. He was so sweet, so young – and so very different from stylish, sophisticated Luke, who always knew what he was doing, what move he was making and what she was thinking. This was different and she decided to enjoy it.

A little while later she gently pulled away from him.

"I have to get back to the party," she whispered, and hand in hand they slipped into the kitchen and then into the living-room, which was now wild with loud laughter and even louder music.

At about ten-thirty some late guests arrived - Georgia, with Michael Wayne, and his daughter Jasmine.

"Sorry we're late, darling," trilled Georgia. "I had to work until nine, and Michael and Jasmine were out of town doing family things all day so they said they'd pick me up at the Malibou." There was something hollow about the way she said it. For a start, Jess knew she couldn't stand Jasmine, and it just didn't make sense for the three of them to be together. And she didn't believe Georgia when she said she'd been working late, because she so often said it. And it was so often a lie.

But she ushered them in anyway, waved them towards the food and drink in the kitchen, and turned to Matthew even more defiantly. The music was sexy and slow and she melted into his shoulders, her face resting against his chest as they danced, her eyes closed against the raging pain and anger inside her.

It was nearly eleven o'clock when the bell rang again. As Thomas opened the front door the music stopped. Jess opened her eyes, her arms still round Matthew's neck, and saw Luke standing on the porch, dishevelled and harassed. It was like being bathed in sunlight. A laser of happiness beamed through her, dispersing all the hurt and anger.

She glided towards him, leaving Matthew alone in the centre of the room. Luke grabbed her hand.

"Jess, darling – I'm so sorry. I couldn't get away, I was on a story the other side of town. It was a police raid and I managed to get into the car with them for the final bust. There was no way I could get a message to you . . . But you know how much I wanted to be with you – you know I'd never let you down . . . Here!"

He pulled a small package from his pocket and handed it to her. "Happy birthday, Sweet Seventeen," he said. She opened it, her hands shaking, to find an exquisite black enamel box painted with white and silver flowers. Inside was a silver bracelet, a linked chain of hearts. She gasped. Luke loved her – he must love her!

Someone was letting loose a cascade of balloons, and everyone was shouting, "Happy birthday!" She was in Luke's arms, her heart bursting with happiness. The music was turned up, the party was banging, her friends were cheering her and, best of all, the boy she loved was kissing her. In that moment of perfect triumph she had completely forgotten all about Matthew, who stood in the shadows abandoned, his face a mask of hurt and betrayal, as everyone danced and laughed the whole night away.

Eleven

It was the morning after the party and Jess was cruising along the road, her face wreathed in smiles. Not exactly cruising, she corrected herself, glancing at the mirror yet again, but at least she was driving. She'd lived here all her life: skateboarded down these roads, roller-bladed down them, biked along them, been driven through them. Now, at last, she was at the wheel – and it felt great.

"OK, then, love," her father cautioned nervously. "You're doing fine, just fine. Perhaps if you could slow down just a *little* bit more when you come to the junction." Jess slammed on the brakes and the car shuddered to a standstill with a shriek of protest. She grinned at her dad triumphantly.

"Like that?" she demanded.

"Er – not quite," he said faintly. "What I think you're going to have to learn is a certain amount of, well, you could call it subtlety. Driving needs to be smooth and gradual, like . . ."

Taking very little notice of her father, Jess had signalled left and was now merrily jerking the car round the corner in little leaps.

"... horse riding!" gasped her dad. "I was trying to say that good driving is like handling a champion mare. Only in your case," he muttered, "it's more like a bucking bronco at a Wild West Show."

"Oh, come on, Dad," teased Jess, swerving round a parked car and waving jauntily at a couple of classmates who stood on the pavement staring at her. "It's only my first time. Give me a break!"

Mr Mackenzie couldn't hide his relief when the promised hour was up and they were back in the kitchen drinking coffee. But he was gallant enough to smile proudly when his wife came in and demanded:

"Well? How did she do? No scratches, I hope!"

"Of course not," he boomed robustly. "She's doing very well indeed. A born driver, our Jess."

"Yup – born to drive people mad!" added Harry, who'd slipped into the kitchen to concoct one of the deadliest-looking milkshakes Jess had ever seen.

"You shut up!" she retorted indignantly. "I'm a great driver! Much better than you'll ever be. At least I know the difference between right and left!"

"So do I, sewer brain!" snapped Harry. In his left hand he

was holding his revolting-looking combination of milk, bananas, peanut butter and chocolate ice-cream. In his right, he carried a computer magazine.

"OK, what's the time then?" said Jess. Harry tipped his wrist to glance at his watch and the milkshake splattered to the floor.

"See!" taunted Jess. "Your right hand doesn't know what your left hand is doing. And you don't either!"

Both their parents were laughing too much to make a fuss about the mess. They were good like that, Jess thought, suddenly feeling rather guilty. Other parents would have gone mad. She fetched a cloth and was helping Harry to mop up the floor when the doorbell rang.

Jess opened the door to see Thomas shuffling on the doorstep. She smiled. "Thank goodness someone normal is here," she said loudly. "I'm having a bit of trouble in the kitchen with a lunatic."

Thomas smiled back and popped his head round the kitchen door to say hello. Jess thought he looked uncomfortable but she couldn't quite work out why. He'd squeezed into the kitchen to help Harry, who was vaguely brandishing a mop. They were punching each other the way they usually did, but his heart didn't seem to be in it.

"I came round to see if you needed a hand clearing up the party," he said.

"Oh, we did all that this morning, didn't we, Jess?" said Mrs Mackenzie. "But it was very nice of you to think of that, Thomas. Look, why don't we get out of your way and leave you in peace."

That was another nice thing about her parents, Jess thought fondly. They knew when they weren't wanted.

Eventually the floor was cleaned, Harry was despatched upstairs to perform an impossible feat on the computer, and Thomas and Jess were alone.

"I didn't thank you properly for the brooch," she said shyly, pouring him some coffee. "It's – it's gorgeous! I really love it . . ."

"That's OK," muttered Thomas. "Thing is, Jess . . ." He was looking even more uncomfortable now, and Jess was getting curious. Of all the people she knew, Thomas was the one least likely ever to feel embarrassed. But he did now.

"It's about last night," he began.

"The party? But it was great, wasn't it? Didn't you enjoy it?'

"Oh, yeah – course I did. Everyone did. Or almost everyone . . ."

"What are you talking about?" Jess wanted to know. She was genuinely puzzled.

"I'm talking about Matthew," Thomas burst out. Surprised, Jess noticed that he was looking quite angry. "You know, Matthew – my friend. Ben's friend. Your supposed friend!"

"Well. What about him?" Jess suddenly began to feel uneasy.

"Look, I bet you're going to say it's none of my business, but I'm going to carry on anyway," said Thomas, gazing intently into his coffee. "I think you behaved pretty shabbily last night and it's not like you. At least, it's not like the person you used to be, before you took up with Luke. Now, I'm not so sure."

Jess stared at him, an icy feeling creeping very slowly up her back. Until this moment she'd forgotten all about Matthew. Now, like a video being rewound, she remembered how angry she'd felt at Luke – and how inviting Matthew had been. She blushed as she remembered how she had nestled in his arms, and blushed even deeper as she replayed the scene in the garden, the long, lingering kiss.

She was speechless. How could she have led Matthew on like that? Then she closed her eyes and shook her head. At the time it had all seemed perfectly logical. Of course she'd abandoned him the moment Luke arrived. It just proved that he meant nothing to her – that she'd been making do with him until the real man in her life appeared. But not for a moment had she considered how Matthew felt about it all.

"I don't know what you're making such a fuss about," she mumbled now to Thomas. "Matthew knew all along that I was going out with Luke."

"Yes, but you hardly behaved as if you were going out with him – or anyone else," snapped Thomas.

"Oh, yeah! So what were you doing – spying on me?" Jess knew she was shouting at Thomas because he was right. She hated being in the wrong.

"I didn't need to," he replied icily. "Whatever you were doing, it was in full view of everyone." He really did sound disgusted – as if he despised her. Jess hated the very idea of that – even more than she hated having hurt Matthew. Even more than she hated being wrong.

"Oh, get real!" she said, trying to sound as cool as possible. "All I was doing was flirting a little. What's so wrong with that?"

Thomas gave her a long, curious look. "Oh, so that's what you were doing was it? Well, as long as you're satisfied it was all innocent fun there's nothing more I can say." Jess was desperate now. Thomas sounded so cold, so adult. It was almost like being told off by a teacher or something. She felt herself beginning to cry.

"OK, OK – I'm sorry," she muttered, not very graciously. "I s'pose I was a bit – um – thoughtless. Have you spoken to Matt at all?"

"Not exactly," Thomas shrugged. "Ben and Molly gave him a lift home last night and he was very quiet. You really humiliated him, Jess – and you must know how keen he is on you . . ."

Jess nodded. It was all too obvious, suddenly, how badly she'd treated him.

"What d'you think I should do?"

"Well – what do you think you should do?" asked Thomas gently. Now it was like being in the headmaster's study; he was pulling all the same tricks.

"Talk to him?" whispered Jess, not much liking the idea. Thomas nodded.

"You've got to, hon," he said gently. "You owe it to him. And besides – think how awful it would be for you both, acting in the pantomime with all this stuff going on between you."

By now, Jess really was crying, and Thomas was melting a little bit. "OK, OK – maybe I was coming on a bit too strong. Come here," he said. He put a brotherly arm round her and hugged her. "It'll be fine as long as you sort it out. Now then, I wonder how Harry's doing with Tomb Raider?"

Thomas stayed for lunch, and spent a couple of hours with Harry, poring over the computer. At about four o'clock he appeared in the door of Jess's bedroom. She was sprawled on the bed listening to Slipknot and doing her homework.

"Fancy going to the cinema tonight?" Thomas asked. "Ben wants to see some Mexican thing with lots of challenging subtitles. But Molly and Ellie were going on about Daniel Craig for some reason."

The old, familiar guilt and confusion spread over her. "Sorry, I can't tonight," she said. "I've got a date." Thomas's face darkened very slightly, but he simply shrugged and said:

"Don't worry. Another time. See you . . ."

For a few moments after he'd left, Jess felt sad. It was as if she was turning her back on her old life and her old friends, even though she knew it was silly to think that way. She wondered if that empty feeling was worse today because of Matthew. It was a shock to think how badly she'd treated him, without even realizing it.

But very soon, her thoughts turned to Luke, and the evening ahead, and all her doubts and sadness began to evaporate. Last night she'd gone from the very depths of despair, when she thought he wasn't going to show up, to the heights of happiness – when he'd arrived with that lovely bracelet, taken her in his arms, and kissed her so passionately in front of the whole party.

That, she knew, had been a turning point in their relationship. He'd signalled to her how much she meant to him. Now, tonight, it would be her turn to show how much she cared.

By the time Luke turned up that evening, all thoughts of Matthew had been banished. Jess was bubbling with excitement. She knew, she just knew, that tonight was going to be special and would herald the start of a new phase in their relationship. She'd dressed carefully – in her favourite black jeans, but with a cool new red jacket, and a red and black skinny jumper underneath.

It was as if her clothes reflected her new sense of hope. Luke clearly appreciated the way she looked. The moment he saw her he gave a low whistle. "You look good enough for the Ritz!" he said at once. "Which is a shame, because that's not exactly what I had in mind for tonight."

Once they were in the car he said casually: "How about coming over to my place? I'm going to cook you the best omelette and chips you've ever had in your life."

"As long as you don't expect me to make the coffee afterwards," said Jess at once. They both laughed.

Then Luke added quietly: "Oh, no – that's not what I was expecting at all." The way he said it sent shivers of anticipation right through her. Luke must have sensed how differently she felt about him now – he knew as surely as she did that now she was ready to give herself to him totally and completely.

When they arrived at his untidy, cluttered flat he fetched a bottle of wine and two glasses. "I don't believe I've really wished you a happy birthday yet," he said, pulling her to him. "I really wanted to get to the party in time to join in the singing and everything. If it hadn't been for that story, and then the drink . . ."

"What drink?" she asked. "I thought you came straight to the party."

"Well, more or less," he said, looking uncomfortable. "But listen, those cops had been really good to me, letting me in on the action. The least I could do was buy them a drink later on, to thank them. I got away as soon as I could, of course."

Jess felt a tiny part of her happiness trickling away. Surely, if he really loved her, he'd have rushed straight to her birthday party no matter what? But she told herself not to be so self-centred. Obviously his work was important. So she decided to play it cool.

"Where did you go?" she asked.

"Oh, the Malibou, I think," he said vaguely. "Yes, that's where it was."

Jess's heart gave a leap. Wasn't that the bar where Georgia said she'd been, earlier that evening, before she and Michael and Jasmine had turned up at the party?

But at that moment, Luke began to kiss her, and all her doubts fled away.

"You are so gorgeous," he murmured. "When I saw you at the party last night, looking so fabulous, surrounded by all your friends, I felt like the luckiest guy in the world."

He looked deep into her eyes and she felt herself melting with pleasure. "It was great last night," he said softly. "But being alone with you is far, far better."

He poured a glass of wine for each of them, and they clinked glasses solemnly as he said: "Happy birthday. I want you to have the best year yet." He led her to the sofa and they sat side by side, sipping their wine. The mood between them was electric. Jess could barely trust herself to speak, she felt so full of love and desire and confusion.

Luke took her hand very gently. "I love you, Jess – you know that." She nodded, her heart pounding with joy. "Are you ready to love me?" She nodded. It was true. More than anything she wanted to be truly his and to make him belong to her.

He kissed her again, a long, intimate kiss full of desire.

"Are you sure?" She nodded again. "Then let's skip those omelettes," he whispered. "I'm going to take you to bed."

Twelve

"What did you want to say to me, Jess?" Matthew was gazing at her with eager eyes which made her heart sink. This wasn't going to be easy.

It was Monday lunchtime. Jess had left a note on Matthew's locker first thing in the morning, asking him to meet her at The Bite, a snack bar near the college, but not near enough to be a regular haunt among the students. Jess had chosen it because she didn't want anyone eavesdropping on her big apology. Now, with Matthew sitting opposite her, she realized he may have had other ideas about why she'd picked somewhere so discreet.

She took a deep breath. "Matthew, I owe you an apology," she blurted out. "I shouldn't have behaved the way I did at the party."

"Correction," he put in. "You shouldn't have behaved the way you did at the end of the party. Up until then I had no complaints at all." He took her hand. "It was the most fantastic evening," he said softly. "You're great, Jess."

"No – no, I'm not," she interrupted. The conversation was going all wrong, somehow. "Look, Matthew – you know I'm going out with Luke. That's why I shouldn't have been with you in the first place."

"Oh, I see," he said, as if the whole truth had just dawned on him. "Of course – you must've felt terrible. Everything had been going so well with us but then, with Luke turning up like that, you had no choice. The party was no place to tell him it was all over." He was actually beaming now. "I must admit I felt pretty terrible when you left me standing like that and went off with Luke. I wasn't sure what to make of it, so I thought I'd give you a couple of days to decide what you were going to do. Now I can see how selfish I was being – obviously you needed time to get straight."

Jess tried to interrupt again but he silenced her. "It's OK, really – I understand. When you're ready, I'll be waiting for you and you've no idea how happy I'm going to make you."

For a moment, at his words, Jess remembered the night before, when she'd lain in Luke's arms, in Luke's bed. As he was about to make love to her he'd whispered: "I'm going to make you so happy, darling – I want so much to make you happy . . ." She sighed. It was no good thinking about that

113

now, when here was Matthew, convinced that she was about to dump Luke for him. How could this be happening?

"You're making this very difficult for me," she said awkwardly. "Matthew, it's not the way you think at all. I'm not leaving Luke. Actually . . ." she blushed, as more moments from the previous evening flashed before her. "Actually, we're more together now than we've ever been. That's what I've been trying to tell you. That's why I wanted to apologize."

Matthew was very quiet suddenly. "So you don't feel anything for me at all?"

"Oh, of course I do! I'm really fond of you. And if you'll forgive me for leading you to expect any more than that, I hope we'll always be—"

"No! Don't say it!" he rasped. "I don't want to hear you say 'just good friends'. That's not what I want and you know it."

"I'm sorry," Jess whispered weakly. "I didn't mean to hurt you . . ."

"Well, don't kid yourself!" Matthew snapped. "I don't break that easily. Sure, I fancied you. When you offered yourself on a plate I wasn't going to turn you down. But since you turned out to be just a little tease I'm recovering very fast. See you at rehearsal."

He got up and stalked out, leaving Jess staring at her baked potato. A couple of tears squeezed down her face. But she knew that she wasn't really sad. Just angry that she'd behaved wrongly. And Matthew wasn't really angry, either. He was just doing his best to cover up his sadness. What a mess, she reflected.

But very soon, she'd pushed all thoughts of Matthew to the very back of her mind. That afternoon Luke was picking her up from college and giving her a driving session. Her father was paying for a course of ten lessons, but that really wasn't enough to get her through her test, so she was determined to get as much practice as she could with anyone who was prepared to take her.

Her heart leapt as Luke drew up outside the college and got out of the car. He made a point of kissing her there and then, right outside the gates. She was pleased, but a bit embarrassed, too. Thomas and Ben were sauntering past them, and she was worried that Matthew might be in the vicinity too. That was all she needed.

But it was good to see Luke again after what had happened the evening before.

"How's my girl?" he asked tenderly. "My own girl." Then, very elaborately, he led her round to the driver's side of his bashed-up little car and opened the door with a bow. "It's all yours, babe," he said, putting on an American accent. "Let's hit the road."

At first things went quite well. Jess remembered what her father had told her about looking in the mirror before driving off, and gently easing the car from gear to gear. At least, that was the theory. In practice, she found that each gear change was rather jerky, and every time the car gave a bounce it seemed to emit a hiccuping noise as well. Luke tensed at every shudder.

"Careful," he said. "We're not at the dodgems now, you know. This is a car, and I'd be grateful if you'd drive it. Not abuse it!"

Jess rattled round a corner and ground to a rather shaky halt.

"OK, OK," she snapped. "I am only a beginner, you know. It's only my second ever go. I thought you knew that!"

"Yes, all right," he said, without much grace. "I'll try and bear that in mind. Come on, let's see if you can get slowly up this hill, using your clutch control."

He was trying to be nice, Jess could tell. But she knew he was tense, and she suddenly remembered something her mother had once told her.

"Never let a boyfriend teach you driving, fishing or card games," she'd advised. "Your father gave me a driving lesson once, and by the end of it we'd practically broken off the engagement!"

Jess wished she'd remembered that advice in time to avoid all this. The more Luke tried to be patient, the more she could tell he was irritated. The more tense he was, the more anxious she became. And her anxiety made her very nervous at the wheel. Time after time she'd slam on the brakes, or make the tyres squeak, or stall the engine.

At last, she decided she'd had enough. She drove home as smoothly as she could manage, which wasn't very smoothly at all really. To crown it all, something went wrong as she attempted to pull up outside the house and the engine stalled.

"What happened there?" she asked, surprised.

To her relief, Luke stopped looking worried. Instead, he burst out laughing.

"You nutter!" he said affectionately. "I might have known you'd get into a spin doing something straightforward like driving. You're amazing. You can do all these things that other people find difficult, like playing the guitar and singing. But give you a simple, practical task – and you completely fall apart."

"That's not true!" she protested. "My dad thought I was pretty good when we went out yesterday."

"Your dad thinks you know how to make the sun shine," responded Luke. He ruffled her hair. "Matter of fact, you probably do know how to do that." And he kissed her, right there in front of the house. Once again, like so many times before, Jess felt her annoyance and her anxiety melt away in the sweetness of his kisses, the excitement that coursed through her when they were together.

"Are you coming to rehearsal tonight?" she asked, as she started to get out of the car.

"Er – no, not tonight. I'm going to be with the band. But on Thursday we're going to start full musical rehearsals. So I hope you've got your routines into shape."

That evening, Jess arrived at the theatre in some trepidation. They were due to go over the transformation scene yet again, which meant that she'd have to face Matthew. Would he still be angry with her? Would he even be prepared to act with her now?

She needn't have worried. Michael Wayne was striding around the stage looking vaguely flustered as he often did. "Right, where's the Fairy Godmother? Where's Cinderella? And where are all the reptiles and rodents?"

"That just about describes me!" said Matthew, sidling up to her. "I've been more of a rat than the part I'm playing. I'm sorry I walked out on you today, Jess – and I accept your apology."

Jess was so relieved that she did a little dance on the stage, ending up with ten cartwheels, one after the other.

"Fairy Godmother! Will you please stop being upside down!" yelled Michael. "Dancing is fine, if you want to incorporate it. The singing's going to be fine. The whip is fine. But cartwheels – they are simply not fine. Fairy godmothers do not cartwheel. Fairy godmothers stay the right way up. Get it? Got it? Good!"

Jess and Matthew started to giggle, and from then on their scene went well. There was the usual happy muddle over the performance with the rats. Everyone knew their positions, and everyone knew that if they didn't keep to them then there was a danger that they wouldn't be behind each other at the right moment. But they all tended to overact and show off. The more the rats misbehaved the more Jess would screech in her Southern drawl:

"We-ell, I'll be darned. Them thar ra-ats think they can slither away from me but let me tell you – they can't!"

"Oh yes we can!" yelled the rats.

Jess turned her back to the imaginary audience and wiggled her hips exaggeratedly. "Oh, no, they ca-an't!" she shrieked, bending down so that her head was between her legs.

"OK, OK!" laughed Michael. "Have it your own way. It's good, it's funny, I'm bored with it, I'm bored with the whole transformation. Let's have a change. Where's Buttons?"

Everyone looked round. Jasmine went backstage to look for Georgia but came back looking puzzled.

"She's not anywhere," she said. The now familiar shadow crept over Jess. And the feeling was confirmed by Michael who said, looking exasperated: "Oh, I suppose she's with the band again, getting even more singing practice."

And getting in even more time with Luke, thought Jess. She

was cross with herself for feeling so jealous. She was the one he loved, wasn't she? She was the one he'd made love to. There couldn't be anything between him and any other girl now.

But still she couldn't quite suppress the nagging doubts that clouded her happiness. For the rest of the rehearsal her spirits were low and somehow the lines she was speaking didn't seem funny any more.

"What's the matter with you?" demanded Jasmine crossly as, for the seventh time in a row, Jess forgot to stand back, arms raised, for the change of dress. They hadn't actually practised this scene properly, with the dry ice. Michael said that could wait for the dress rehearsal. But what was meant to happen was that while the dry ice swirled round the stage, Jasmine would rush into the wings, put on her ball gown, and rush back in time for the spotlight to beam away from Jess and on to her. It was, naturally, her favourite moment in the whole show and she hated Jess for spoiling it.

"I suppose you're worried about your precious boyfriend getting all matey with Little Miss Buttons," she said cattily.

"Course I'm not," Jess retorted. "I'm actually worried more about the lizards and the rats. Come on, let's do it one more time." And, as bravely as she could, she did her very best to shout out her comic lines, while inside a knot of worry was winding all round her heart and threatening to break it.

Thirteen

The college gym was empty – except for two figures, one leaning against the other at a precarious angle. The upright one was Jess. The other, tilted in a straight line as if drunk, so that his head reached just below her shoulder, was Thomas. They were quite still, frozen like statues.

"Hold it, hold it, hold it – OK stop!" he said after a few moments. He slithered up again and gave her a triumphant grin. "That was fine – much better!" he added. "Now, four or five more times and it's a roll, as they say in showbiz."

Jess groaned. "Slave driver!" she accused him. "I thought it was a little help you were offering, not a gruelling night of personal Olympic training! Anyhow, I thought you said I was doing all right."

"You are, you're fine." Thomas looked at her appraisingly, his nose wrinkling as it often did when he was thinking hard. "At least, most of it's fine. I just can't figure out why you seem to be having such trouble with this one routine. It's not as if it was particularly difficult, but I get this sense that your body is refusing to perform properly for you, as if you were inhibited about something. And that's definitely not like you."

Jess flushed and felt alarmed. Thomas knew her too well, that was the trouble. She'd asked him to go through the dance routines with her because they hadn't been going too well. And last night's rehearsal had almost been a disaster.

This was the only choreographed dance that she had to do in the show, apart from a few very easy slapstick routines with the mice and rats and lizards. Although she hadn't had any formal dance training she hadn't expected to have any problems. Inside her, she knew it wasn't the dancing that was the problem at all really. It was her partner. Thomas, as usual, had got right to the heart of what was bothering her.

Michael had decided that when the Fairy Godmother and Buttons had their touching scene together, after Cinderella had swept off to the ball in the magic coach, they should add a little dance to the duet they sang together. Jess had never quite got used to the toned-down version of the song. She much preferred the raunchy country style that she used when she first appeared to Cinderella. She resented having to make it prettier for Georgia, who had a pretty voice but nothing like as strong as Jess's.

As far as Jess was concerned, that was hard enough. Now she

had to perform a jolly little dance during the musical break of the song which involved stepping arm in arm with the one girl in the world she really didn't feel like hugging. Even worse, the whole thing ended with Buttons, straight as a poker, tilting across the stage as if falling to the ground, and landing instead on her shoulder. And last night she'd felt herself rebelling. Every time they tried the dance and Georgia began to fall towards her she'd panic. At one point she stepped backwards so that instead of landing on her, Georgia collapsed on to the floor.

"What is the matter with you, Jess?" she'd demanded crossly, rubbing her side. "It's perfectly easy. At least, it is for anyone who knows anything about dancing."

Michael ran his hands wildly through his hair, looking exasperated. "Look, love," he began patiently, "we're not asking a great deal. Just relax, let Georgie fall down towards you and at the moment of impact you can support her from behind. That way you won't need to worry about the impact."

The more he advised her and Georgia taunted her the more stiff and awkward she became. It was terrible. And it would have been even worse if Thomas hadn't been there. Michael called a five minute break and then said, quite threateningly for him, that they would have one more go at the dance routine and he expected it to go smoothly.

Jess sat slumped backstage, sipping hot chocolate from a flask and feeling miserable. She just wasn't used to messing things up. It was so galling! This whole scene was meant to be the Fairy Godmother consoling Buttons because the girl he loved had no feelings for him at all. She'd rushed off in all her finery without even saying goodbye to him. In fact, the Fairy Godmother could barely bring herself to touch Buttons because he – or rather she – may well be stealing her own boyfriend!

"You're getting into a panic over nothing," said a gentle voice beside her. It was Thomas, who crouched down, took her drink without asking, and helped himself to a few sips of the hot chocolate. "Look, if you try to relax for the last part of the rehearsal, I'll go through the whole thing with you tomorrow if you want."

Jess brightened at once. "Would you? Would you really? That'd make all the difference." Then she looked crestfallen. "But how am I going to get through it tonight? I'm hopeless – I really am. Maybe we should just drop the dance. The song's OK."

"Don't be crazy," said Thomas. "It's a pantomime. You've got to have a dance. But try not to take it all so seriously. You've got a great character there – just carry on thinking you're the Queen of the Silver Dollar, forget about yourself, and whatever you do forget that Buttons is really Georgia. That's what real actors do."

"Don't you mean Georgie?" snarled Jess viciously. She hated it when people like Michael called her that. It was as if they were part of her magic circle. Most of all, she hated it when Luke called her that.

"Come on, Jess, she's not so bad," said Thomas. "I reckon she's just a bit off with you because you give off these terrible unfriendly vibes. You need to loosen up, you know." He pulled her to her feet and squeezed her hand. "But if you can't manage that, just stick with the acting. She's a lovelorn kitchen boy and you are a country mama who can steer horses and kill rabbits and make apple pie . . ." He tailed off then, but Jess was laughing and beginning to feel much better.

So, with Thomas's help, she'd managed to get through the dance. It wasn't brilliant. She was still rather stiff and inhibited. But she got the steps more or less right, she put her arm round Georgia's waist without flinching and she even managed to catch her at the right place at the end.

It was quite late by then and Jess was exhausted. She was also feeling anxious. Luke was due to pick her up at the theatre and drive her home. She was very glad he hadn't been there to witness her appalling performance during the dance, but now she was beginning to look round anxiously and the usual knots were forming in her stomach.

She had pinned so many hopes, more than she'd even realized, on the idea that if only she and Luke became lovers then everything would be perfect. She wouldn't be plagued by jealousy and doubts and he, in turn, would have no reason even to look at other girls. She would be all he needed or wanted. So far, though, very little had changed. He loved her, she was sure he did. But, if anything, she felt even more unsure than she had before.

Suddenly, all the lights went out. There was a hush, followed by shouts and a hubbub of voices. And seconds later the whole auditorium was alight with darting sequins of fire. At first Jess was dazzled by the flashing lights and general chaos. Then it dawned on her. Of course! Tonight was Bonfire Night, and the lights were sparklers. Very soon Luke was beside her, thrusting more sparklers into her hands as he kissed her.

"Let's light up the place first," he whispered. "Then I'm going to take you home so we can light up the night." Jess shivered with excitement and pleasure. This new phase of their love affair was full of promise and adventure. Luke was loving, sexy and considerate. Yet still she couldn't banish the foolish doubts that pricked her in a thousand places, just as the sparklers were stinging the darkness.

Everyone was milling around the stage and the theatre. Michael was shouting rather nervously that they should be careful, that he wasn't sure if the theatre was insured for this kind of thing. But no one took much notice. They were having fun and sparklers, after all, were indoor fireworks.

They cast a rather eerie light over the place. No one quite looked like themselves, and as everyone was playing with the sparklers, writing their names in the air and waving them above their heads, you only occasionally caught glimpses of people's faces. Jess spotted Thomas, laughing and teasing some of the girls in the cast. And Ellie, who'd arrived with Max at the same time as Luke. The two of them seemed to be getting on very well and were kissing as they linked arms, their faces bathed in the glow of the sparklers.

Once Jess saw Georgia's face, lit by what looked like a bouquet of fire. Luke was holding the sparklers and saying something in her ear. Georgia was nodding and laughing, her face glowing strangely in the unreal white dancing lights.

At that moment there was a sudden flare, turning the white light to bright orange. Georgia's raucous laugh became a piercing scream. A spark had somehow caught a strand of her hair, and set it alight. Like a fuse, the flame shot right up to the top of her head. There were a few seconds of confusion. But that was all. Luke came to the rescue. He simply pulled out a handkerchief and damped the flame with it, hardly seeming even to rush. His calm action put out the fire at once, and seemed to soothe Georgia, who collected herself quickly, and smiled adoringly at Luke.

"OK, OK – that's enough!" Michael was instantly by her side, his face contorted with anxiety and irritation. "You're all right, aren't you? You're sure you're all right?" he asked her. Then, his arms flapping in all directions, he suddenly started shouting at everyone. "That's enough! I knew something like this would happen. Come on, everyone – let's wrap it up here. Next rehearsal, Sunday night. And don't forget, it's our first rehearsal with the band."

A very short while later, Jess was in Luke's arms, in his bed. He was making love to her, and she was clinging to him, her every thought and all her desires wrapped up in this moment of longing and loving. Yet even as he murmured her name, and whispered how much he wanted her, an unwelcome picture flashed into her mind. Even at that moment, she remembered Luke, standing close to Georgia, the two of them laughing, Georgia gazing up at him adoringly as he rescued her from the flames.

Now, with Thomas's arm round her shoulders, and hers round his waist as they stepped through the dance routine yet again, Jess found herself reliving those strange, tormented thoughts. The joy and ecstasy of being with Luke; the torture of wondering about Georgia. And, yet again, she tripped and stepped on Thomas's toe.

"Look, you're not trying," he said, pretending she'd really hurt him. He hopped round the gym a few times faking agony. "Let's do the song again, then go into the routine. I'm not giving up until you're perfect, so you might as well make an effort."

He put the music back on again at the place where the band struck up Jess's theme tune.

It's the magic – the magic of love
A love that has to be true
And if you – if you truly believe
Then one day it will happen to you.

They were standing arm in arm as they harmonized the chorus. Thomas was a good, strong singer, and Jess thought the song had never sounded quite so good. It was so nice to be singing with him that she found it quite easy to put her arm round him, and lead him into the simple dance steps that had been giving her so much trouble.

Strangely, Jess was sorry when the finale was over. They'd held their pose, and now Thomas was straightening up and moving away from her.

"See, I told you it was easy," he said gruffly. "You shouldn't have any problems if you do it like that."

"I think I know the trick," she told him triumphantly. "I'll just pretend it's you pressing up against me instead of Georgia, and I'll be fine." She gave him a bright, flirty smile. "I might even enjoy it."

Thomas didn't look at her. He was busy packing away the laptop. "Yeah, well, anything that turns you on," he muttered.

"Just remember I'm here if you need me." Jess felt oddly sad as she and Thomas wandered home that evening and he gave one of his funny waves at her door. She just couldn't work out why.

Fourteen

Jess had begun to settle into a new routine. There was college every day of course, and rehearsals on Tuesdays and Thursdays, as well as at the weekends. She saw Luke most weekends and at least twice during the week, though she still had her eleven o'clock curfew except on Saturdays. Luke was always teasing her about it.

"I wish you wouldn't go on about my Cinderella complex!" she'd complain. He'd usually just nuzzle her neck or kiss her tenderly, and say affectionately: "It's only because I can never get enough of you. Why can't you just tell your mum that I'll promise you get to bed on time, as long as you're with me?"

Jess would always laugh along with him but at the same time she felt uncomfortable. Most evenings that they spent together they would end up making love and she would feel closer and closer entwined with him, almost as if they were the same person, the same body. But then he'd drive her home, abandoning her on her front doorstep, and off he'd cruise on his own, living a late night life while she battled with delayed homework and early nights. She couldn't help wondering where he went afterwards and who he saw but she had decided not to ask or probe. Luke hated the idea of being cross-questioned, as he put it. She just had to pretend that everything was fine.

The worst times were always after rehearsals. Jess was convinced that Luke would be back with Georgia the minute he'd dropped her home. She had no proof, of course, she just felt it. And she'd pick up on every little hint, every possible nuance, and interpret it as more evidence that there was something going on between them.

Her insecurity and all her suspicions came to a head one Thursday evening towards the end of November. It was the very first rehearsal with the band. Before that, they'd had to make do with a recording. So this was an important moment, especially as it was the first time Luke had heard the duet performed by Jess and Georgia.

Jess had made up her mind that she just had to make the scene a success. And at first all her hard work seemed to be paying off. She remembered everything Thomas had taught her – singing heartily with Georgia, gazing at her fondly just as a Fairy Godmother should do, dancing the jaunty little steps arm in arm, and forcing herself to relax for that last moment, when Buttons fell across the stage and landed just beneath her chin. She thought she'd really pulled it off.

Then Luke's icy voice cut through the auditorium. "It doesn't work!" he announced. "That duet is going to have to change."

"What – what do you mean?" stammered Jess.

"Well, for a start, your voices aren't balanced properly. Georgie's too quiet, you're too screechy, you're just not balanced properly."

"Oh, no!" Georgia murmured in Jess's ear. "I knew it! It's because my voice isn't as strong as yours. I'm too reedy!"

Privately, Jess agreed with her. But that didn't seem to be what Luke meant at all.

"You're just going to have to tone it down, Jess," he said. "Harmonies don't work if one voice dominates the other. And besides . . ." This was the bit that really hurt her. "Besides, you're coming on far too strong. Try and bring out the melody, a bit more like Georgie does. I want this sweet and lilting, OK?"

Jess was scarlet with humiliation. How could Luke have criticized her like that? And how could he prefer Georgia's anaemic little performance to her own full-blooded one? But there was nothing she could do or say – not in front of the whole cast, and certainly not in front of Georgia.

She just had to stay on stage, suppressing all her natural power and strength in order to match Georgia's soft, pretty little voice.

Later, she tried to tackle Luke about it. "I don't know why you had to be so horrible," she said. "It wasn't as if I was all that bad. You could have talked about it afterwards or something . . ."

But Luke couldn't see why she was so upset. "I thought you'd want to be treated like a professional," he said. "You wouldn't catch a real performer making a fuss about a simple little direction."

"It wasn't a simple direction!" she stormed. "You just told me I was rubbish in front of everyone. OK, so maybe you do think I'm vulgar and over the top and not sweet-sounding enough. Well, I'd far rather be me and too loud than some other people who are subtle and boring and can't even hold down a tune!"

She didn't really mean to criticize Georgia so directly, but she'd been genuinely stung at Luke's comparison between them. She wondered whether he'd defend Georgia now, against her spiteful words. But all he said was:

"OK, sorry, love. I didn't mean to put you down. Let's talk about the weekend . . ."

He broke off, his face a picture of guilt. "Oh, no – I forgot! I'm on assignment this weekend. I'll be in Manchester until Sunday at the earliest. But I can come and pick you up and we can spend the evening at my place."

"Oh, no we can't!" rejoined Jess, still smarting from their

134

row. "As a matter of fact I won't be around on Sunday night. We've got a gig, a proper gig with real loud music and I'm going to sing properly for once, the way I want to! And no one's going to tell me to tone it down because guess what? People like it the way I do it. Right?"

Luke looked rather astonished at her outburst, but he grinned good-humouredly.

"I keep telling you, you're talented in lots of ways. I love the way you sing in the band, it's great. Tell you what, I'll give you a ring when I get back from Manchester and we'll spend some time together before your gig. Some real quality time." He kissed her tenderly and she melted against him. So what if he made her feel unsure of herself sometimes? It was worth it, for all the good times. After all, lots of girls would give anything for a guy like Luke, she told herself. Someone who couldn't wait to get her alone, to kiss her and make love to her.

The Sunday night gig, at a youth club near the college, was their first for ages. The pantomime was eating into everyone's time so they'd only managed one quick rehearsal and they weren't adding any new numbers to the repertoire. They'd arranged to meet at six o'clock, two hours early, so that they could practise one more time and get the sound right.

By early afternoon Jess was in her now familiar state of

confusion. She was looking forward to the gig. As she lay in the bath, letting rip with all her favourite numbers, she realized how much she'd missed the pure, unadulterated high of being on stage and belting out loud, heavy, wild rock.

But her excitement was mingled with anxiety. She wanted to see Luke. She needed him – needed to know that everything was all right between them after that stinging row. If only he'd get back early – if only he'd ring now to say he'd be over right away because he couldn't bear to be parted from her for another moment.

But he didn't. Two o'clock ticked slowly by . . . three o'clock came and went. Jess brushed her hair obsessively and piled it into an even wilder style than usual, with silver scarves and spikes. Then she squeezed into a new, short black dress that looked like leather when she was on stage, but felt like satin.

It was four-thirty when Luke finally showed up. Jess flung a big coat over her band clothes and rushed out of the house as soon as she saw his car. As she opened the passenger door Luke grinned: "Not so fast, Miss Daisy. I thought you were supposed to be the driver round here."

Jess was a little disappointed. Of course, she was pleased to get any practice she could, since she was only getting two professional lessons a week. But she'd had a rather different idea about how they were going to spend this precious time together. And she'd hoped Luke had been thinking along the same lines.

And of course, because it was Luke sitting next to her, watching her every move, she kept making mistakes – jerking the little Peugeot in a series of bumps and gear crashes until he finally lost patience.

"I thought you said you'd done three-point turns!" he snapped.

"I did – I can do them really well with my teacher," she protested.

"Some teacher," he sneered. "Seems to me you don't know the very first rule."

"Which is?" demanded Jess, unsuccessfully attempting to restart the engine.

"If you want to impress your boyfriend, don't mess with his clutch!" he retorted. "Come on, Jess, let's go home. I want three kisses for every time you stall my engine." Then he grinned and ruffled her hair affectionately. "I keep telling you, love – stick to what you're good at. It doesn't matter if your driving's a bit dodgy as long as you can set me on fire the way you do."

"You don't have to be so patronizing," protested Jess furiously. But then he leaned over and kissed her, and her anger evaporated away as it always did.

"Let's go back to the flat," he whispered. Jess looked at her watch and gasped. It was half-past five. "I've got to get to the gig," she said.

"Oh, come on – just a quick coffee," urged Luke. "I'll get you to the gig, don't worry."

When they arrived at the flat, Jess slipped off her coat. Luke took one look at her and drew in his breath sharply. "That is some dress," he murmured, pulling her into his arms. His hands slid down the shiny, skin-tight fabric, snaking along the contours of her body. "Oh, God, Jess – you are so sexy!" he groaned, covering her face with hot, searching kisses.

"Luke – I can't," Jess protested. "I told you I've got to get to the gig by six." But Luke simply held her even tighter, his body pressing urgently against hers as his hands roamed up and down her back. There was just one brief moment of doubt, as Jess remembered the others, waiting for her at the youth club. She should really be there first, because it was her turn to set up the sound system. And in any case, they were relying on her for the final practice.

But somehow, as she twined her arms round Luke's neck and sank into his scorching embrace, nothing seemed to matter but his passion, his desire, his overwhelming need for her.

It was nearly two hours later when Jess finally arrived at the club. "I'm sorry everyone – I'm really sorry!" she panted as she rushed in. The other three were on stage and Thomas was singing. He stopped abruptly at her arrival, his face a mask of fury.

"Oh, don't worry," he spat. "We were managing perfectly without you. After all, we're beginning to get used to the kind of person you've become. But don't think you can stay in this band if you can't even bother to show up on time."

Ellie looked worried, Ben embarrassed. Thomas was so angry that he couldn't even shout at her. He just quickly told her the running order of the songs and ignored her when she tried to apologize for being so late.

She played her heart out for the next two hours. It was the best way of drowning out her anguish about Luke. And she was trying to make up to the others for letting them down so badly.

She went really crazy during their final number, which was a very beaty version of "Baby Come Back" – she played a wild guitar solo, then gyrated round the stage to Ellie's screaming saxophone. As they screeched out the final notes, the audience burst into a frenzy of clapping, whistling and stamping.

Afterwards, though, there was still a definite frost in the atmosphere and Thomas was still studiously ignoring her.

"Look – I really am sorry, I couldn't help it," she tried to say. But Thomas shook her hand off his shoulder and refused to be placated, even though Jess went out of her way to do more than her usual share of coiling up the wires of the sound system and putting away speakers and instruments.

"Coming for a coffee?" said Ellie, the peacemaker, when it was time to leave. Jess took one forlorn look at her three best friends, now ranged against her. She shook her head sadly.

"Not tonight – I don't somehow think I'm wanted." And no one tried to come after her as she made her own, lonely way into the deserted street.

When she got home that evening, she popped her head round the living-room door to say good evening. Sitting next to her mother on the sofa was Mrs Manley, her hand full of a sheaf of documents.

"Hello, dear," she said with an ingratiating smile. "Just the person I wanted to see. I was showing your mother these sponsor forms, they're to raise money for the local hospice. All you need to do is go without your favourite foods for a month, and you get people to sponsor you per item per week. So you see someone could pick chocolate, or butter or something and put down, say, a pound for every week that you did without it. Isn't it a marvellous idea?"

"As long as no one suggests I do without my own creature comforts," added Jess's dad, pouring himself a whisky. Mrs Manley shot him a disapproving look.

"I'm asking your mother if she'll help out by distributing a few of the forms among her circle, which," she added with a little sniff, "is rather different from my own. And it would be simply wonderful if you could help out too, dear. I'm trying to get my Georgia involved and of course she'd love to but she is just so busy these days. That hotel is working her all hours. Next Thursday she has to leave work for rehearsal, then go back to the hotel for the night shift. Honestly . . ."

But Jess didn't hear the rest of the monologue. A piercing pain shot through her. She remembered so clearly what Georgia had been saying last time she'd seen her. Michael had asked if everyone would be available for the following week's rehearsals because they'd be concentrating on the songs. Georgia had said: "I'll be there all day if you need me, we're having such a slack time. Two conferences have been cancelled for next week – if I'm not careful they won't be needing me at all."

So she'd been lying! She wasn't working late at all. In fact, she was working less than usual. So where was she going after rehearsal on Thursday? And where would Luke be after he'd dropped her off home at eleven o'clock?

Fifteen

Jess lay awake all night, fretting about what she'd heard and going over the same pattern of thoughts again and again. So what if Georgia was lying to her mother? Why was that any business of hers? Then unwelcome images would flash into her mind of Luke's face close to Georgia's; his hand putting out the flame of her hair; the two of them laughing together.

Then Jess would remember the good times with Luke: the way they laughed together; their passionate love-making that afternoon, when he'd told her over and over again how much he wanted her; the way he looked at her when she was singing . . .

And that, of course, reminded her of how quick he was to attack her singing these days, and how anxious to protect Georgia. It all seemed to piece together so neatly, she tormented herself. Then she became outraged, at the thought of how only this evening she had betrayed her friends, nearly wrecked their gig, broken the most basic trust for a man who probably wasn't even being faithful to her.

And as she tossed and turned in the darkness, assailed by the crossfire of her tortured thoughts, Jess knew she would never have any peace of mind until she knew for sure what was going on between Luke and Georgia, and why Georgia was telling all her lies.

By the next day, Jess had made a plan. It was wild and hazardous, but it was the best she could think of and it gave her a sense of purpose which would help propel her through the next four days until she could carry it out.

But they were four very difficult days. Jess felt as though she was in a daze most of the time, drifting through her days at college without really taking much in. It was as though she was in the grip of an obsession. All she could think about was her plan for finding out the truth – a plan so secret she couldn't even tell her best friends. And she wasn't even sure how many of those she had left.

"Seeing Luke this week then?" Ellie asked one day.

"Er, no – not till Thursday," replied Jess.

"What's up? Have you two had a row or something?" Ellie asked curiously.

"No, of course not," snapped Jess. "What d'you mean?"

"Oh, come off it, I am supposed to be your best friend,

Jess. So I sort of notice when you're not right. Shall we begin with Sunday night?"

Jess looked wary. "Look, I've said I'm sorry about that. I know I let you down badly."

Ellie sighed. "I didn't bring this up to get at you. I'm worried, that's all. It's just not like you to behave like this. And I want to help. So shoot!"

Jess felt tears dart to her eyes. She so longed to pour out her heart to Ellie. But this time, she knew she had to keep her secret to herself. So she decided to hint at some of what was troubling her.

"Oh, I suppose this pantomime is getting to be a bit of a strain," she admitted. "You see, when Luke first saw me I was singing with the band and he really seemed to be impressed. Now, with this song I have to do, he's so critical of me . . ."

"Oh, well, everyone knows why that is," scoffed Ellie. "It's because Georgia can't keep up with you. Your voice is so much better. It's obvious to all of us in the band."

Jess looked at her sharply. "Does she practise that much with the band, then?" she asked at once.

"Well, she did for a while," said Ellie. "But now you come to mention it, she hasn't been around that much for rehearsals lately . . . Hey, wait a minute, Jess – you're not still jealous of Georgie are you? I thought we'd gone through all that ages ago."

Jess forced a watery smile. "Oh, no – of course not. Not really. I just, er, just wondered why everything has to be adjusted for her – even if it makes the show worse, that's all."

"It won't make it worse," said Ellie. "You're both good, but the song won't sound right unless your voices are balanced. Honestly, Jess, that's all there is to it. Luke's crazy about you, not Georgie. So chill out, will you?"

But Jess couldn't chill out. She went through her days in a dream, her eyes glittering strangely, her face hot and feverish. And each night she lay awake, plotting and fretting as the day of reckoning drew nearer.

"Are you OK, love?" her mum asked at breakfast on Wednesday morning. "You're looking very flushed. Sure you're not coming down with something?"

Exhausted and shivery after a string of anxious days and sleepless nights, Jess looked at her mother blankly for a few moments.

"Erm, nothing really," she muttered. Then she thought better of it. "Actually, Mum, I'm not feeling all that great. Didn't sleep too well . . ."

"You've been working too hard, dear," said her mother, looking worried. "All your studies, and the pantomime on top of everything. Look, I'm not going in to work today. Why not stay at home with me and have a rest? You'll make yourself ill if you don't let up a little."

145

So Jess allowed herself to stay in bed all morning and be spoiled by her mother. In the afternoon, she said brightly: "I'm feeling ever so much better now, Mum. And you know what would really cheer me up?"

"What, darling?" asked her mother, who was sipping a cup of tea and catching up with *Neighbours*.

"How about giving me some driving practice?" Jess suggested. "It's ages since I had a go in Dad's car, and it's so much nicer than the driving-school old wreck."

With the Volvo waiting tantalizingly just outside the house, she was all too aware that a bit of extra practice was just what she needed. Jess's dad had been away for a few days and had left the car. So she gazed cajolingly at her mother and added: "Besides, it'd be lovely to have you sit with me for a change. Everyone else is so critical."

She was right, too. It did cheer her up to be in the driving seat, with her mother chattering away next to her. Mum was great like that, she reflected. She just assumed you knew what you were doing and let you get on with it. It was almost like driving without anyone at all breathing down her neck. At the end of their outing Jess was feeling much more confident about her driving, and much happier, too, about everything she'd decided to do the very next day.

"I may not be here when you get home tonight," her mother said the following evening as Jess was getting ready to leave. Great! she thought, pinning her beloved guitar brooch to her jacket collar.

"Oh, really?" she remarked, trying to sound bored. "Will Harry be OK?"

"He'll be fine. I'll just be distributing a few more of those wretched sponsor forms. I wish I'd never agreed to help out."

At the rehearsal, Jess was quiet and tense. For most of the evening they were rehearsing some of the ball scenes which didn't involve her. Luke was vaguely helping out with the music although he didn't really have a lot to do either. So Jess sat in the stalls, watching him, wondering about him, feeling strangely detached from him now that she was so close to finding out whether he was cheating on her.

She and Georgia were only needed tonight for the finale, when the whole ensemble gathered on stage to sing a reprise of *The Magic of Love*. Still feeling as if she was watching herself going through the motions, Jess acted and sang more forcefully than usual, grabbing Georgia by the waist and joining in the general upbeat spirit of the chorus. Thomas was right, she thought. It really does work, imagining that you are someone else.

"You're awfully quiet tonight, hon," remarked Luke, as people started to leave. "You OK? I mean, do you fancy going out for a coffee or something? Haven't seen you for so long – I've really missed you this week."

147

"Well, I am a bit tired," admitted Jess. "Would you mind if we didn't go anywhere? I think I just need to get home and have an early night."

She could have sworn that a look of relief passed fleetingly over his face. Of course! she thought triumphantly. If he gets me home early that leaves him more time to get back to Georgia! Everything was beginning to piece together now.

She was silent as Luke drove her home. He kept glancing at her, looking concerned. It was only just after half-past ten when he pulled up outside her house. "You're sure you're OK?" he asked tenderly. Jess nearly laughed out loud at his audacity. He actually sounded concerned, as if he really cared about her. Little did he realize how she'd seen through all his tricks, his lies, his deceit.

Well, he wasn't the only one who could put on an act. She turned to him and smiled sweetly. "I'll be fine, as long as I get a good night's sleep," she said. Then she leaned over and kissed him caressingly on the lips. "Maybe you should get to bed early yourself," she added lightly, while inside she was thinking scornfully: *Yes, that's exactly what you'll be doing, you and Georgia. Only tonight, you're going to be found out once and for all!*

After she left him and let herself into the house, everything went surprisingly smoothly. Her mother was still out, which was very convenient. As an extra precaution, she deliberately picked a fight with Harry about who was going to use the bathroom first, and made a great display of having to get to bed. By five to eleven Harry was in bed, her mother hadn't come home, her father, of course, was still away. It was very easy to slip downstairs and out of the front door. Not even the cat noticed she was gone.

She did experience one or two qualms as she let herself into her father's precious Volvo and slid into the driver's seat. He'd been so trusting to give her that special key of her own. She had a momentary qualm – then quashed it. How could anything be more important than her moment of discovery – her unmasking of Luke and his terrible deceit?

She tuned in to Radio One and popped a bag of pear drops into the glove compartment. Might as well make myself at home, she thought.

Jess loved the feeling of power that filled her as she started the engine and began to drive down the street. It was so exciting to be in charge, completely in charge, with no one telling her what to do. And, even better, she had a mission to accomplish.

A few minutes later she was pulling into Georgia's road. There was the big double-fronted house. There was Georgia's little green car. And – yes! There was Georgia herself, at spot on eleven o'clock, carefully closing the front door and stepping down the path. She took for ever to strap herself into the car and start the engine. At least, it seemed that way to Jess, skulking just a few yards behind her in the darkness. But eventually, Georgia pulled away from the kerb, unaware of the dark, silent shadow behind her.

Jess was so tense that she could only think about one thing: keeping on Georgia's tail, following her through the quiet back roads and on to the main highway until all her secrets were uncovered.

When they reached the open road, Georgia quickened her pace. Jess did, too. They were driving along the main road that led out of town and towards the hotel. Jess felt a momentary panic. Suppose she really was going to work? Suppose all her suspicions had been madly, crazily wrong – and Georgia was simply off to do her job, just as she'd told her mother she was.

Then, suddenly, she signalled left. Jess, just a short distance behind her, did the same. Georgia turned into a side road and drove a very short distance before she pulled up outside a pub. A tall, rangy figure emerged from the shadows and right up to Georgia's car. Georgia leant over to open the passenger door. He bent down and, with a blinding flash of anguish and fury, Jess saw them lock into a long kiss.

And that was the last thing she saw before the sudden bang, the tinkle of glass, the heavy jolt . . . and then everything turned black.

Sixteen

"Jess! *Jess! Are you all right?*" Through the blackness and then the dizziness as she began to return to consciousness, Jess was aware of a familiar voice calling her name anxiously over and over again. Confused and sick, she tried to open her eyes, then quickly closed them again as the world seemed to rotate precariously round her. Something was wrong. She knew that deep voice – would have known it anywhere. But why wasn't it Luke's voice? Where was Luke?

"Luke . . ." she murmured weakly.

"He's not here," said the voice. "Look at me, Jess, and tell me you're OK." With great difficulty Jess forced her eyes open and found herself gazing into the pale, worried face of Michael Wayne!

Horror washed over her in huge waves. It must be a nightmare, she thought wildly. She was still only half awake, and only slowly began to piece together what must be

151

happening. There were so many awful things that her addled brain decided to deal with them one at a time, in order of importance.

"My dad's car!" she managed to moan. "Have I – has it ...?"

"Don't worry about it," soothed Michael. "You're OK, that's the most important thing."

Jess suddenly became very agitated – so much so that she began to forget the pain in her head and the sick feeling that engulfed her.

"What do you mean, don't worry?" she demanded, sounding almost like her old self. "How can I not worry? I wish I'd been hurt, anything, just so long as the car ends up in one piece." And then, quite suddenly, she burst into tears – great wracking sobs which only reminded her of the terrible mess she was in.

"It's not bad, honestly," Michael soothed her. "Just a buckled bumper."

"Really?" sniffed Jess eventually, her tears beginning to dry up.

"Oh, and ... erm ... a couple of head lamps," Michael added. She burst into tears all over again.

"Look, Jess, I think we'd all better have a little talk, don't you?" suggested Michael wearily. He disappeared for a moment, then returned to the car and made Jess move into the passenger seat. "Coffee first," he announced. "Then I rather think we've all got some explaining to do."

He was silent as he drove back to the main road, on the tail of Georgia's little green car, and then to the hotel. Disjointed thoughts raced through Jess's mind. What was he doing with Georgia? Where was Luke? And what, oh what, was she going to say to her father about his beloved car? And about the trust she had broken so violently?

The first thing she noticed as Michael led her into the coffee bar in the hotel was the cool, almost icy figure sitting waiting for them. Georgia was gazing intently at a menu and barely glanced up as they joined her. Jess was puzzled. But then, everything about this ghastly night was rather unreal.

"Now, how are you feeling, Jess?" asked Michael gently.

Jess gulped. "Not bad," she conceded. "I – I don't actually feel ill or anything, just a bit shaken up."

"Well, you certainly had us worried," said Michael heartily. "Didn't she, Georgie?"

Jess winced involuntarily. She so hated it when people called Georgia that. Especially tonight, when she was being anything but cute and cuddly.

Georgia gave a slight, imperceptible shrug. Jess got the distinct impression that if anyone had been worried about her, even for a second, it probably hadn't been Georgia. A scuff mark on her new boots would have worried her more. Or a slight change in the weather.

"Anyway, I'm fairly sure it's nothing very serious," Michael continued, still desperately trying to sound cheerful. "I think you just fainted from shock, and it always feels terrible afterwards. But you're not concussed or anything. Thank goodness you were wearing your safety belt or you might have done yourself a bit more damage. Not that you were going very fast . . . But driving straight into the back of a stationary vehicle isn't exactly recommended in *The Highway Code*, you know."

"I know," agreed Jess dolefully. "I've been reading it every night in bed, studying for the test."

"You – er . . . What did you say?" Michael looked aghast.

"Yes, that's part of the problem," Jess said tonelessly. "I'm still a learner. And apparently it says in *The Highway Code* that they specially don't recommend driving into the back of stationary vehicles if you haven't passed your test."

Michael's face had turned from pale to sheet white. Georgia's expression had not changed at all.

"I think it's time we ordered the coffee," she drawled.

They sat for a while in tense silence. Then, when the coffee arrived, Michael said:

"Right, time for some straight talking. What were you doing driving along that country lane all by yourself, late at night, without, it transpires, a licence?"

Jess took a deep breath, and then blurted out the truth. The whole truth. How she'd begun to suspect that Luke was more interested in Georgia than in her. How she began to piece together all the evidence until she became quite convinced that they were seeing each other secretly, late at night, having a torrid, passionate affair.

"It was driving me crazy," she wept, the tears splashing into her coffee. "I just got fixed on this one idea that I had to catch them in the act and prove that I was right. It sounds stupid, I know it does." She looked earnestly at Georgia, whose face was now even more an expressionless mask. It was hardly inviting, but Jess plunged on regardless. "I'm sorry, Georgia, I really am. I can see I got it all wrong. And I should never have gone spying on you."

"Think nothing of it," Georgia remarked drily, sipping her espresso. Jess was furious with her for acting so calmly in the middle of such a drama. A little bit of her was rather impressed, too.

"Well, er – I think after all that," said Michael, obviously distressed, "we owe you a bit of an explanation, too." He looked anxiously at Georgia but her face remained blank.

"Jess, I wouldn't want – well, neither of us would want this to go any further, as I'm sure you'll understand," he blustered. "But as you can see . . ." He waved rather ineffectually towards Georgia. Jess stared at them, first one and then the other, as light after light began to dawn.

Of course! Georgia had been lying to her mother, but not

because she was seeing Luke. It was Michael she was seeing. Michael she was hanging around for after rehearsals. Michael she was waiting for, all those evenings she chose to spend with the band. Jess suddenly remembered the night of her party – how Georgia had arrived with Michael, late at night . . .

"You know how it is," Michael confided. "You can't explain love, it's just that magic something that happens between two people. You see, Jess, I took on the pantomime because I was going to be at home for a while and because I really wanted to give something back to this community, after all it had given to me."

Jess was glazing over, hardly listening, but then she thought, just maybe, he was trying to tell her something important.

"Between you and us," he continued in a confiding tone, "I wasn't all that happy about the baby. I mean, obviously, I couldn't have been that happy or I wouldn't have started . . ." He broke off, then, and gave Georgia a really soppy look that reminded Jess of the look Luke sometimes gave her when they were out together with a bunch of his friends. It was a sweet, adoring look – but somehow she'd never quite trusted it, and always preferred him to be argumentative and teasing and sexy and silly, the way he was when they were alone. Fleetingly, she wondered if

Georgia felt irritated by the look, but then she squashed the thought. Georgia, she reminded herself, simply didn't have feelings.

"Anyway, I got involved with the pantomime and of course I was knocked sideways by all you talented luvvies." He flashed a smile. Jess, obediently, attempted a smile in return. After all, she told herself guiltily, he was her director.

"But then this – this gorgeous vision turned up," he went on, turning to Georgia. She looked bored. Jess looked interested – she couldn't help it. "I'm a man of the world, you know," he explained condescendingly. Jess again remembered things that Luke had said, to show her how much more he knew about the world than she did, than she ever could. She smiled, helplessly.

"So I fell in love," Michael finished simply. "Or, to be accurate, we fell in love. It was wrong, we knew it was. But when something like that hits you, like a thunderbolt, like a flash from the sky, you can't resist. It would be wicked to resist, I think, in a way." Jess continued to smile, her face frozen. But privately she was thinking that he was laying it on a bit thick. Surely he could have just said he fancied Georgia like mad and couldn't resist her?

"And now we're in so deep," he explained earnestly. "We can't stop, Jess. Can we, darling?" Georgia performed another of her immaculate shrugs, and turned her attention to the dark chocolate mints which had arrived with the second round of coffees.

"So we'd both be very grateful indeed if we kept this as a little secret between the three of us," Michael was saying. Jess had so many new thoughts whirling round her head that she was finding it difficult to concentrate on anything. But through the blur she was aware that Michael was explaining how difficult this all was; how his wife was expecting a baby and although it was Georgia he really loved, of course he did, well he just couldn't afford to upset poor Marjorie at a time like this. Jess even thought she heard him muttering about what bad publicity it would be, if it ever came out that he'd been seeing another woman while his wife was pregnant.

"I'm sorry?" she said. "You're worried about *publicity*?"

Michael didn't seem to notice the irony in her voice.

"Naturally," he nodded. "I'm known as a family man, after all. My biggest telly appearance was playing the husband in *Love Letters*. It could ruin me."

Jess was amazed that he could so callously admit that his image, his public image, could be more important to him than honesty in his private life. She stared at him, open-mouthed, her own pressing problems temporarily forgotten.

Michael clearly misunderstood the appalled look on her face.

"So I'd really do a great deal to avoid any, er,

unpleasantness," he went on. "This car business, for example. Why don't you let me handle it, Jess? Your father will be in bed by now, won't he?" Jess stared at him dumbly, feeling rather out of control.

"He's away until tomorrow," she whispered.

"Right, here's what we'll do," said Michael quickly. "I'm going to tell him everything is my fault. I needed the car desperately tonight because – um – because mine broke down and I had to be on a TV programme in Birmingham. People always think that being on TV is an emergency . . . So I persuaded you to lend the car to me, and unfortunately I had a little argument with, let's see, the BBC car-park gate. That sounds nice and glamorous, doesn't it? And of course I'll get it mended, it'll be good as new, I'll see to that . . ."

Feeling shaken and bemused, Jess allowed Michael to drive her home. She slipped upstairs, exhausted, knowing that the next day a whole fabric of lies would be put in motion, just to protect the guilty: Michael, who'd betrayed his pregnant wife; Georgia, who, without any regard to the fact that he was married, had entered into a full-blown affair with him; and Jess herself. A criminal, she reminded herself, as she tossed and turned on her pillow, her face burning and her heart pounding. She had broken the law; broken the trust of her father; risked lives, in the pursuit of her mad, groundless obsession. And now she was about to allow Michael to make

159

everything all right again – to paint over all the cracks – just so that all three of them could carry on with their lies and deceit.

As she sank at last into a fevered sleep, Jess wondered if she could really go through with it. Should she let Michael put his plan into action? And if she did, would she really be able to live with herself afterwards? The last thought of all, as she drifted into her troubled dreams, was of Luke. Luke had turned out to be blameless in all this misery. He'd been telling her the truth all along. So when his chiselled face, his familiar smile, his long, lean body flashed into her mind, why didn't she feel the old surge of happiness and warmth? Why, instead, was there a shadow where all that joy used to be?

Seventeen

"Jess! *Jess, are you all right?*" The insistent voice penetrating through her troubled dreams startled her into confused consciousness. Where had she heard those words before? Memories of the tinkle of glass, the blackness, the awful sick feeling flashed back to her in a jumble. Was she still slumped at the wheel of her dad's car? Was it Luke's voice urgently calling her name? No, of course, it hadn't been Luke, had it? But it certainly didn't sound like Michael . . .

Jess forced open her eyes to see her mother's anxious face close up to hers, her mother's hand smoothing away her hair and touching her burning cheek.

"Hello, Mum," Jess mumbled rather blearily. At once, her mother's face cleared and she smiled with relief.

"At last!" she said. "I've been trying to wake you for ages. It's way past getting up time, and I couldn't get a peek out of you." She peered suspiciously at her daughter with that

161

special mother kind of look. "Hmm . . . as I thought. You're not well, are you, love? I thought you hadn't quite recovered after you took the day off on Wednesday. You looked a bit peaky then, but now . . ." She reached over and laid a cool, practised hand on Jess's forehead. "Definitely flu," she pronounced, and rushed off to fetch the thermometer. "I knew it, I just knew it . . ."

Jess lay back on the pillows, watching the room spin round. So that was it! She was ill. Maybe all those memories were feverish nightmares, she thought in a wild moment of optimism. Maybe she'd been delirious, and none of it had really happened at all. But no – she knew she wasn't all that ill. It had been real all right – the drive through the night on Georgia's tail, the shock of seeing that kiss, the crash, and then the realization that it wasn't Luke Georgia had been seeing at all, but Michael . . .

After Jess's mum took her temperature and gasped worriedly at the verdict, she'd given her a hot drink and two aspirins.

"Try and get some sleep now, love," she advised in that special gentle voice that took Jess way back to her childhood, when a word and a kiss from Mum could fix just about anything. "Your dad's coming home from his conference this afternoon," she added. "See if you can get a bit better to welcome him back."

162

If only she knew! thought Jess, her head pounding as if it was going to crack in two. Just the thought of her father and what she had done to him was enough to send her fever sky high!

All morning, she drifted in and out of a troubled sleep, terrified of what the day would bring. At lunchtime, her mother arrived with some soup on a tray.

"That actor Michael Wayne rang this morning," she announced excitedly. "You know, dear, the one who's helping out with your pantomime. He wants to know when your father will be home. Said he'd like to pop in and talk to him this evening. Strange," she mused. "I wouldn't have put him down as someone who'd be all that keen on double glazing. And he sounded as if it was quite urgent, too . . ."

Jess sat up at once, startled. "Oh, it's not about double glazing!" she blurted out. "At least – well, I'm fairly sure it wouldn't be that." She found her voice tailing away and her mother looking at her strangely. She knew it was her moment to speak, but somehow she just couldn't. Instead, she began coughing – at first, to cover her confusion, and then for real, such dry, wracking coughs that her mother became quite alarmed and forgot, for the moment, what Jess had been saying.

Word seemed to have got around that Jess was ill. The doorbell kept ringing all afternoon. First, a panting, anxious

Ellie arrived, rushing on her bike in between lessons at college.

"Are you really ill?" she demanded, getting to the point at once, as she usually did. "Or is this what those of us in the know like to call an emotional ailment?" To her immense shock, Jess burst into wild, uncontrollable tears.

"What is it, Jess? It's not Luke, is it?" Even at the height of a drama, Ellie found it difficult to suppress her curiosity. And for once, for the first time in ages, Jess found herself talking to her best friend – really talking, the way best friends should. She told her everything – about how jealous she'd been of Georgia, her master plan to find out the truth, and then, finally, the quite unexpected secret she'd uncovered. Ellie was speechless, her eyes as wide as CDs.

"Wow!" she kept saying in a breathy voice. "Wow! Oh, Jess, that's amazing. But you know I did keep trying to tell you she wasn't seeing Luke. She's OK, honestly. I like her." Jess remembered how silent and cool Georgia had been last night, even when Michael was saying how much she meant to him. She'd hardly glanced in his direction, and she certainly hadn't said a word to Jess.

"Anyway," added Ellie, who always liked to look on the bright side. "It's turned out pretty well, hasn't it? I always knew Luke was nuts about you, and only you. And now you've proved it, haven't you?"

164

Jess shook her head sadly. "Not really," she croaked, exhausted from the combination of flu, tears and anguish. "I've proved he's not seeing Georgia. But I still don't know where I stand with him, Ellie. And it's really hard . . ."

Ellie gave her a hug, and thrust a magazine and a Mars bar into her hands.

"Look, I keep telling you – don't worry, everything's fine. I mean – you don't even have to do any explaining about the car, do you? Michael's going to get you off the hook. Get well again and you'll soon realize how lucky you are."

Soon after she'd gone, a whirlwind appeared in her doorway. It was Harry, just home from school.

"Hi, you don't mind if I don't get too close, do you?" he greeted her. "Yuk! It's true! You really have got the plague! Mum! Mum! Quick, she's got great purple blotches all over her and some of them are bursting and blue kind of stuff is spurting out . . . !"

"OK, OK! I don't care if you are doing the Tudors and Stuarts this term, that wasn't very funny!" rasped poor Jess. "What do you want? Why are you here? No reason? Good, then get out. I mean, you wouldn't want to catch your death in here, would you?"

"Nothing, no, course not!" squealed Harry merrily. "Did you ever see *The Killing of Sister George?* No? Pity. So true to life. Oh, by the way, you don't mind if I send this by air mail, do you, as I'm too sensitive to get close to the dying." A large, blue envelope whizzed into the room and on to Jess's pillow as he scooted away.

Sighing impatiently at the awfulness of little brothers, and hers in particular, she tore open the envelope. Inside was a beautiful picture of an old-fashioned circus, alight with performing elephants, dancing horses, clowns, lions, the flying trapeze . . . Who could it be from? She squinted for a few seconds at the terrible handwriting before she managed to make any sense of it.

Get well soon! We need you back in the ring. Love, Thomas.

She should have been pleased, or at least relieved. Thomas hadn't spoken to her at all since the night of the gig, and she'd begun to worry that maybe he never would again. So this peace offering should have cheered her up. But for some reason, the fever she supposed, tears were rolling down her cheeks again, and she was sobbing into her pillow. Why was everything such a mess, just when it should all be so great? She'd just dozed into another fitful sleep when she was woken by yet another interruption, the sound of voices downstairs. Her stomach turned over as she managed to make out her father's bluff, cheerful tones as well as a deeper, richer voice which boomed through the ceiling. Michael Wayne!

Painfully, her head still throbbing, Jess forced herself out of bed and on to the landing. Her legs were rather wobbly so she sat at the top of the stairs and listened to the snatches of conversation which wafted her way.

"So very sorry to cause you inconvenience," Michael was saying. "I wanted to come and talk to you right away. You see I was in quite desperate straits last night. I had to go to the studio after our rehearsal . . ." Jess could hear him explaining how he'd had to rush to do an interview at the BBC and his car had broken down.

"You really mustn't blame Jess, Mr Mackenzie," Michael was saying in his most charming, seductive voice. "She was acting on the most generous of motives, truly she was."

"But if she wanted to lend you the car, why didn't she ask me?" That was Jess's mum, sounding very puzzled.

"Oh, she tried," Michael assured her expertly. "At that particular time of the evening you were out, and I was, you see," now his voice was apologetic, and very suave, "I was in the most frightful hurry."

"It's true I was out for a bit," Jess's mother agreed uncertainly. "But only for a very little while, giving out those forms. Why on earth didn't she mention it later on when she got home?" There was just a little pause, and then she answered her own question. "Of course, I was forgetting," she said, sounding relieved. "She wasn't well. She still isn't well, not at all well. She must have flopped into bed with that awful temperature, poor love."

Jess knew she should be feeling pleased that the story seemed to be working, but she couldn't help feeling uncomfortable. It was as if she was allowing Michael to make a fool of her parents, as well as tell lies on her behalf. As she crept shamefully back to bed she could hear Michael explaining smoothly how sorry he was to have damaged the bumper. How he'd had it all sorted out, at his own expense of course. It was perfectly all right now, but he hadn't liked to deceive them, that was why he'd had to come and straighten it all out there and then.

"Hey!" hissed Harry from her door. "Is that him? *The* Michael Wayne? Can I get his autograph, do you think? Do you suppose if I went down now and had a word with him he'd give me some advice about how to get copyright for my computer songs?"

"Harry – just shut up, will you," groaned Jess wearily. She didn't even have the spirit for her usual level of insult. The most irritating thing about Harry right now was that although he was a pain, he was a relatively innocent, well-meaning pain. While she was steeped in dishonesty and sleaze. "Shut up and get to bed and give me a break!"

"OK, OK! Chill out, sister. Anyone would think you were ill or something." He put his head round the door daringly. "Or maybe you're just sick at heart." And off he slithered, leaving Jess shivering in her bed, wretched with fever and guilt.

It wasn't long before the voices calmed down and the front

door opened and shut, after a brief exchange of courtesies. A few minutes later Jess heard her father's familiar footfall creaking up the stairs and into her room.

"Daddy!" she cried weakly. And then she was in his arms, sobbing like a baby all over again.

"It's OK, love," he kept saying as he hugged her. "Don't fret. You were silly to lend Mr Wayne the car but it's OK, he's explained everything. There's no need to get so upset." He held her for a very long time as she sobbed her heart out.

At last, her face still buried in his strong, comfortable shoulder, Jess realized she couldn't allow the lies to go on. This was her dad, after all. And unless she came clean now, things would never be quite the same between them again. She'd always carry with her the knowledge that she'd deceived him.

So as her tears began to dry and the sobs and the coughs subsided, she managed to whisper in a very small voice: "Dad – Dad, there's something I've got to tell you." And once she started blurting out her story, it seemed as if she was never going to stop.

Eighteen

"It wasn't quite the way Michael told it," she began hesitantly, quaking inside. Her father was looking at her expectantly and she nearly backed out. Then, heart in mouth, she said quietly: "I don't know how to tell you this, Dad, but I know I've got to." She took a deep breath, and once she'd started she gabbled out the whole story, stopping only to gulp down her tears and cough out her sobs.

"I know, love," her father said simply, when she'd finished.

"What?" she gasped. "What d'you mean?"

"I knew he was covering up," her father explained wearily. "I was just waiting for you to tell me yourself."

"But – but how?" she stammered, amazed. After all, she had decided to come clean because she couldn't bear the deceit. Not because she'd had any idea at all that her father had seen through the whole thing.

He reached into his pocket and brought out a packet of

pear drops. "Not what I normally carry in the passenger seat," he explained drily. Then he scrabbled in the other pocket and produced the little guitar brooch that Thomas had given her, the one she always wore for good luck.

"It was under the driver's seat," he told her. "But your mother had seen you pinning it on for rehearsal last night. You're not very good at lying, love, are you?" She'd shaken her head, then, silent with shame and embarrassment.

"Don't you want to hear the rest of what happened?" she'd finally whispered.

"No, I've heard enough," her father said quietly. "But there may be more you need to say to me."

Jess forced herself to look into his eyes, and she didn't like what she saw. Her kind, easy-going father was staring at her with an expression she'd never seen before: cold, icy contempt.

"Dad?" she whispered, barely able to speak. "Oh, Dad, I'm sorry. I think I must have been crazy to do what I did. I – I suppose you'll never trust me again, will you?"

"Well, what would you feel if you were me?" he asked sternly. It was an old trick that he'd often used before. He even sometimes asked her what punishment she thought she deserved. Now she thought hard before answering.

"I'd be really angry about the car and about me driving without a licence," she admitted. "In fact, I'd probably have

171

me locked up or something. . . But I think I'd be glad that I'd told the truth."

His face softened. "Well, I think maybe I'm getting my little girl back after all," he said gently. "Jess, I think you know how serious this is, and I think you're suffering, aren't you? This fever of yours – I get the feeling it's tied up with that Luke of yours, and whatever has got into you has driven you to this madness."

Jess nodded, her eyes filling with tears.

"But at least you've come clean and told me the truth. Because the one thing I couldn't bear is lies. And I suppose it must have taken some courage to own up to last night's bag of tricks."

She nodded again, and noticed that some of the ice in his eyes was beginning to melt. And then he was hugging her, and she was crying again and whispering, "I'm sorry, Dad, I'm really, really sorry," over and over again. "I don't know what got into me," she sobbed. "I suppose I was just so hung up about Luke I lost all my senses."

Her father kissed her head very softly. "Well, at least you trust me enough to tell me the truth. You didn't try to blame this flu thing, did you? You didn't even think of pretending you'd done all this because you weren't well. I can give you credit for that. And I do believe you're sorry. Anyway, thanks to your director chappie the car's going to be fine. And most important of all, no one was hurt. So one way and another I've a good deal to be thankful for."

Warmth and relief were flooding through Jess. At least the lies were over now, and her father still loved her. "You do know why you felt so ill after your little bump, don't you?" he added. "It's just a touch of flu. The doctor was quite adamant that there were no signs of concussion, not even a bruise. Thank goodness you were wearing your seatbelt."

"You – you mean you actually checked with the doctor?" Jess was beginning to feel as if she must be in a dream again.

Her father nodded. "Well, we knew you must have been involved somehow, so we had to check up. I'm just very, very glad you decided to come out with the truth, all on your own." He hugged her again before getting up to leave her. When he got to the doorway he turned round again.

"Oh, and by the way," he said. "Next time you decide to abscond with my Volvo, do remember that I object very strongly to having the radio tuned to Radio One. That was the biggest give-away of all."

She managed a watery smile. "I'll remember to make it Radio Two next time, then you'll never pin it on me." Registering his smile, she continued hopefully: "So – so you'll forgive me? We can forget it ever happened?"

"Oh, sure," her dad replied kindly. "You're grounded till the end of the year, but apart from that, everything's just fine."

Of course Jess felt much, much better now. But she was still unwell, still very guilty, and still in a state of turmoil about all that had happened. More than anything, she found herself thinking about Luke. Where was he now? Surely, if he really loved her, he'd have found out by now that she wasn't well, and flown to her side?

Later that day, she couldn't be sure when, the doorbell chimed into her anxious fretting, and a visitor was invited into the house. She heard footsteps climbing up the stairs and her door was opened.

"Someone to see you," said her mum softly.

And in walked, of all people . . . Georgia herself, bearing a little bouquet of roses and a basket of goodies from the Body Shop.

"Hi," she said awkwardly. "I heard you weren't well, and I really . . ." She turned round to make sure that Jess's mum had left the room and closed the door behind her. Then her face changed dramatically – from polite and embarrassed to fierce and intent.

"Jess, I really, really need to talk to you!" she hissed. Jess could only stare at her in astonishment. She was beginning to think she'd had a few too many surprises lately. But this was the most unexpected yet. Cool, cold, icy Georgia was gripping her urgently by the wrists, her cheeks red, her eyes glistening with tears.

"You see, you're the only one who knows. I've been keeping it to myself for so long, and it's just getting so hard. Jess, what do you think? You saw us together! I'm not cross, really I'm not! I know I was a creep last night, but that was only because I was so upset. You see, Michael wants it all to be a secret, but – but I love him so much. I was glad you found us, honestly I was. It made it seem more real, somehow. Less of a dream. And I couldn't say anything because I knew it would only make him angry or something. So tell me, how did it look to you?"

Jess had never seen Georgia emotional or passionate. It was a completely new side of her. And she couldn't help responding to it.

"Well, it looked to me as if he was crazy about you," Jess began, moved by the look of hope and gratitude in Georgia's eyes. And as she heard herself speak, she remembered all the times that Ellie had used exactly the same words to her about Luke. She, too, had always found them comforting. But at the same time, she'd never really quite believed her. After all, how could anyone, even a friend, really know what was going on between two lovers.

"It certainly looked that way," she corrected herself. "But I'm not the person to ask. I mean – I hardly know either of you—"

"Yes, but that doesn't matter," Georgia interrupted her

175

urgently. "You know about us, and you're the only one who does. You've got to tell me—"

Suddenly, Jess felt wise – weary, but wise. "You've no idea how much I'd like to make you feel better," she said slowly. "But it's much better to tell you the truth. And that is that only you know how it is between you. Nothing anybody on the outside can tell you means anything at all. So why are you asking me?"

And now it was Georgia who had tears streaming down her face, as she began to pour out her heart to Jessica. How she hadn't meant to get involved with Michael – of course she hadn't. She wasn't very proud of the fact that she was seeing a married man. But then, he'd been so insistent, so sure of himself. He'd told her his marriage was over. The baby was a mistake, and he'd be leaving as soon as he could, but he wasn't going to do that before it was born.

Then she was sobbing even more uncontrollably. "I believed him!" she cried. "I thought he loved me! He came on so strongly to start with. He was irresistible."

"You must have been very flattered," Jess put in faintly.

Georgia gave her a strange look. "Why did you say that?" she snapped.

"Oh, only because I know exactly how you must have felt," Jess replied. She felt a mysterious affinity with Georgia, which made her reach out and squeeze the other girl's arm. "He must have seemed like the perfect man for you – except he's not, is he?"

Georgia shook her head sadly. "No, I guess not. These last few weeks have become hell, you know. At first, he was desperate to be with me – he'd do all the running, be wherever I wanted him to be, arrange everything round me. But it's not like that any more. I have to hang around waiting for him after rehearsals, and pretend to my mum that I'm working. And then there are all those maybe nights. You know – he might be able to get away, he might not, I have to wait for him to ring. I have to pretend not to mind if he can't make it. I suppose I'm just kidding myself that I really matter to him . . ."

She'd been talking as if to herself, but then she seemed to remember Jess and gave her a penetrating look. "But it's hardly the same between you and Luke, is it? I mean, I know I flirted with him a little, but that was only to put everyone off the scent, because Michael was so paranoid about being found out."

"He seemed pretty jealous about the two of you," Jess couldn't help remarking.

Georgia shrugged. "Oh, well, that's men for you. But Luke's sweet. And it's obvious that he cares for you, Jess. I mean, I'm sorry if I made it look like anything was happening between us, but I didn't mean it that way. He's so crazy about you!"

"Yes, well, I'm sure you're right, and I'm really, really sorry

I behaved the way I did," Jess burst out. It was true. She suddenly liked Georgia very much indeed. In fact, she felt as though the two of them had been through something very, very similar. And that was why Georgia's assurances about Luke meant no more to her than Ellie's, no more to her than her own could possibly mean to Georgia. When it came to love, only two people could know the truth.

"Thanks for coming to see me," Jess said warmly. "I really do appreciate it. And, er – your secret, it won't go any further."

"No, it definitely won't," Georgia assured her grimly. "Because it isn't going to be one any more. I'm finishing with him, Jess. You've made me realize just what a fool I've been, and I'm not going to put up with it any longer."

For some reason, Jess finally drifted into a long, peaceful sleep after Georgia had gone. Everything, somehow, seemed to be falling into place. And when she woke up, she felt so much better that she managed to get up and make her way very carefully and slowly downstairs that afternoon.

Her mum had gone to work; Harry was out. She was alone, bundled in blankets on the sofa, when her next visitor arrived. It was Luke!

"Jess! I'm so sorry. I had no idea you'd been ill. I was out of town on a story and I was going to ring you the minute I got back but then I just ran into Ellie down town and she told me, so I rushed on over."

He scrabbled in the shoulder bag that he'd flung onto an armchair. "Here, I've brought something to cheer you up."

Triumphantly he handed Jess a tattered plastic bag. Inside were two CDs, one a blues compilation and the other the latest Grace Hari album. Typical! Jess thought bitterly. Fancy giving music to someone with flu. As if her head wasn't pounding enough already!

Then she softened. It was sweet of Luke to get the CDs for her, even if they were probably freebies from work. And after all, he hadn't known then that she was ill.

So she smiled, and melted, and then she was in his arms again, the old familiar longing flooding through her. The tingle ran down her spine as his lips pressed against hers. The shiver of excitement as he wrapped her in a long, passionate embrace. There was no doubt about it, Luke was a gorgeous guy. But now, for the first time ever, something had changed.

As he lifted his face from hers and gazed deep into her eyes, she realized what it was. For some reason, probably because of all that had happened since they'd last been together, all that she'd suffered, worried about, thought about, fretted about, she wasn't asking herself the same questions any more. She wasn't really wondering any longer how much he loved her, or whether he loved her at all.

Suddenly, instead, she found that she was wondering how much *she* loved *him*. Or even if she'd ever really loved him at all.

Nineteen

It was never quite the same again between Jess and Luke, although it took her a little while to realize what had changed. They still saw each other regularly. They even went to bed together and he was as loving and as indulgent as ever. It wasn't Luke, after all, who had changed. It was Jess. Instead of regarding Luke as someone to look up to, to learn from, to please – she had started to see him as an equal. And somehow just a little of the shine had begun to wear off.

It all became clear on the day of the Dress Rehearsal, a few weeks later. There had been a mad scramble to get everything ready by the beginning of December. Most of the costumes had been hired, but a team of helpers, including some unlucky mothers, had been roped in to put together the rest and to make any last-minute additions. Another team had painted backcloths and scenery, but key members of the cast had been put in charge of collecting extra props for particular scenes.

Jasmine, of course, had opted for the ball scene, and had had a wonderful time scouring second hand shops and the attics of various aunts in search of gilt-legged chairs, fans, feathers and general glitter.

Jess – typically, she thought sardonically – was allocated the kitchen. At first she'd thought it very boring, but in the end she'd amassed an array of extraordinary items that would give the kitchen scenes character and even humour. She was particularly fond of an old Women's Liberation poster belonging to her mother. It was a huge picture of a dustpan and brush and it proclaimed in stark black letters: HOUSEWORK IS DRUDGERY. Jess thought it would look hilarious pinned above the mantelpiece where Cinders would sit scrubbing and weeping.

She'd found a broom, of course, but she was also very proud of a very ancient Hoover donated by her grandmother, who hadn't ever had the heart to throw it away. "I always thought it belonged in a museum, dear," she'd said. "But I suppose the stage is just as fitting. Oh, and you might as well have this while you're about it."

"This" turned out to be a very heavy old pair of bronze kitchen scales. Jess loved them. They were huge, and came with their own set of weights. When Michael saw them he was delighted. "We'll put something silly on them, just to get the audience in the right mood!"

"How about the heavy side is women's work and the light side is men's work," suggested Ellie.

"Too political," Thomas said at once. "How about a bunch of lizards? That would sort of imply that they were a normal part of kitchen equipment."

"No, I think there should be a great big red heart which is heavier than all the weights," put in Jasmine.

"Or the heavy heart is a woman's and the light one is a man's." That, of course, was Georgia. She said it lightly enough but Jess, glancing at Michael, saw him flush with embarrassment, or it might have been annoyance.

"No, it'll have to be onions," he declared, clearly anxious to change the subject. "And we could put in a few jokes about tears, and smelly breath."

"Yes, maybe the Fairy Godmother could offer Buttons a packet of Polos to solve his most intimate problems," quipped Thomas. And they'd all laughed.

But the Dress Rehearsal was to be the first time that everything – backdrops, lighting, props and, of course, costumes – would be brought together on stage for the whole performance. They'd set aside a whole Sunday. Everything was to be brought to the theatre first thing in the morning, and Michael had said they should be ready for the performance by late afternoon.

The final turning point for Jess came that morning, soon

after she'd arrived at the theatre in a state of high excitement. Everyone was laughing and chattering as backcloths began to be lowered and raised, costumes appeared as if from nowhere, and in all corners of the auditorium there was frantic activity.

Luke was going through the final score with the band. Jess was doing a mad warm-up routine with Georgia. Suddenly Michael announced: "OK, props on stage please."

Jess's hand shot to her mouth as she let out a horrified gasp. "Oh, no! You're not going to believe this. I've forgotten them."

"You what?" said about a dozen people at once.

"I'm sorry," she said. "I really am. I don't know how I could have done anything so stupid. I guess I had other things on my mind last night . . ."

She shot a pleading glance over at Luke. He knew exactly what she meant. They'd been together the night before, and they'd made love. He'd dropped her home late and she'd rushed to bed, tortured by her usual turmoil of emotions. So surely he'd help her out of this mess now.

"Typical!" he said in a lazy voice that managed to be cutting at the same time. "You're hopeless, Jess, you really are. I'm amazed you remembered to turn up at all. In fact, it's fairly extraordinary that you know which planet you're on. You certainly seem to be occupying a different one from the rest of us."

183

There was an awkward silence as everyone waited, astonished. There was no mistaking the cruelty of Luke's words, even though he'd tried to make them sound, as usual, like a big brother teasing a favourite little sister.

Jess could feel the blood draining from her face. Her first reaction was to flinch with humiliation, as she had done so often in the past when he had criticized her. But then something else took over – a pure, white anger at Luke. How dare he put her down in front of everyone like that? How dare he put her down at all? She wasn't incompetent or forgetful, not really. She just seemed to be that way when she was with Luke. He expected it. Almost, she realized suddenly, he wanted it.

"What did you say?" she demanded icily. The room froze.

"Oh, come off it, Jess – haven't you caused enough problems?" he said lightly. She knew he was trying to pretend that this was just an affectionate little tiff. But she wasn't going to let him get away with it. Not this time.

She walked slowly and purposefully towards him. It seemed to take for ever, especially as everyone in the world was watching her.

"You really do have a problem, you know that, Luke?" she spat. "You're not better than anyone else, or cleverer or cooler. You're just a professional put-down! And I can't for the life of me see any reason why I should put up with it any longer."

Luke flushed with embarrassment. "Don't make a scene, hon," he said uncomfortably. "You're just upset that you forgot the props and held everyone up. So why don't you just run along and get them and we'll all chill out."

"No problem," she said in a very quiet voice. "I'll go and fetch them now. It won't take long . . . And by the way, you patronizing piece of, of . . . of pond weed!" She cast Luke a look of cold contempt. "Don't you ever, ever speak to me like that again. Understood?"

And she flounced past everyone and out of the door, her heart racing but her head held high. Angry and upset, she charged down the road with such force and purpose that it was a few minutes before she became aware of footsteps running after her and a voice calling her name. It was Thomas, who finally caught up with her, panting heavily.

"Jess, couldn't you hear me shouting at you?" he demanded between breaths. "I'm coming with you. I – er – I thought you might have too much to carry."

Jess thought she had never in her life been so pleased to see anyone. It had been tough walking out of that theatre alone. What she needed now was a friend. Thomas was far too tactful to mention Luke, or the awful scene. He just chatted about the Dress Rehearsal as though nothing much had happened and Jess quickly found herself relaxing. It was always fun, being with Thomas.

They managed to get a bus back to her house, where the props were stored, and it wasn't long before they were on their way back again, staggering under the weight of her eccentric assortment. Thomas carried the weights balanced precariously on his shoulders, a broom in one hand and a large clock in the shape of a fried egg in the other. Jess had the vacuum cleaner, a large tea towel bearing the legend "A Present From Blackpool", and three large plastic jars. One said *Bread*, one said *Sugar*, and the third one said *Flowers*.

"Where did you get those?" demanded Thomas, intrigued.

"Oxfam shop," gasped Jess, concentrating on balancing everything at the same time.

"You mean – someone actually owned them?" Thomas started laughing. "I think there must be some crazy person somewhere who invents things like that just so people will give them away . . . and then eventually they'll end up where they belong, in pantomimes."

"Oh no, I think what it is, is that nasty things have to be made so you can give them to people you don't like," said Jess. And while they waited at the bus stop they played a game, thinking up suitable presents for undesirable people.

"A calculator that plays 'God Save the Queen' when it gives you the answer – that's for Mr Robbs," said Thomas. Mr Robbs was his maths tutor.

"Bath salts that smell of onions – for Jasmine," said Jess.

186

"Oh, yeah – and how about your friend Georgia?" asked Thomas boldly.

Jess blushed. "Well – actually she is my friend," she admitted. "I like her. I didn't use to but I do now."

At that moment the bus arrived. The driver took one look at the pile of strange objects on the pavement. "Upstairs," he said curtly.

"But – but there's rather a lot . . ." protested Jess.

"And they're quite heavy," added Thomas.

"You're lucky I'm letting you on at all," replied the driver, unimpressed.

Somehow, they managed to get everything upstairs with them, and by the time they flopped into their seats they were laughing uncontrollably. People were giving them some very strange glances – and they could both perfectly well see that they made a very odd pair indeed.

They were still giggling when the bus arrived at the nearest stop to the theatre, and they both scrambled down the stairs with all their clutter. Thomas was so weighed down that he hurtled down the stairs and right off the bus, straight into Jess, so that they ended up sprawled over the pavement in a tangle of kitchen equipment.

"You OK?" asked Thomas as he pulled her to her feet. She nodded, then noticed that he hadn't removed his hand. Then she noticed she didn't really want him to. They were standing very close, then he was pulling her towards him. And right there, in the street, surrounded by all the crazy kitchen props, he kissed her.

It was a gentle kiss. Almost the kiss of a friend. But at the touch of his lips an electric charge rushed through her. And then it was over. He gave her a hug, and muttered: "Come on – better hurry up with these." Then he immediately tripped over a wire which had escaped from the Hoover, and this time Jess had to pull him to his feet. They were both giggling now, but there was something else in the air. Something that Jess had never noticed before.

"Hey – you two need any help?" Ben and Molly appeared from round the corner.

"We thought we'd offer to help, since we're kindly making up the audience this evening," explained Molly.

"And they sent us off to look for you," Ben said, and then stopped in amazement as he took in the clutter around them. "You're mad! You brought this lot on the bus? Totally, completely barmy!"

In the end they spread the load between the four of them, chattering and laughing as they swayed down the road in a crazy crocodile line. As they made their way into the back door of the theatre, Jess reached out for Thomas's hand and squeezed it hard.

"Thanks," she whispered. "You're a real mate."

"Jess . . ." Thomas said, his hand still firmly in hers.

"What?" Her heart was pounding as their eyes locked together. It seemed very quiet, in that dark empty corridor, and for some reason she was holding her breath.

"Oh, nothing," Thomas answered quickly. "It was nothing. Any time you need a – a helping hand, you know where to come."

Then he pulled his hand away from hers and hurried away from her and into the crowd backstage. For a moment or two Jess stood and watched him disappear round the corner. Then she followed, wondering why she suddenly felt so utterly bereft.

Jess never knew how she managed to get through the Dress Rehearsal that day. She tried to act as if nothing had happened, of course, but she couldn't help noticing that Luke was icily ignoring her and that just made her react with even more determined cheerfulness. She threw herself into the show, bounding round the stage with such abandon that Michael had to tell her to calm down and save herself for the real thing. And all along, deep inside she was in turmoil.

At the end of the rehearsal Luke approached her grimly. "Lift home?" he offered. Numbly, Jess nodded and followed him out to the car. He drove in silence, his jaw set sternly. Once, Jess reflected, she would have been thrown into paroxysms of anguish at this display of cold rejection. Now, it didn't really bother her.

"So – aren't you even going to say goodnight?" she asked lightly. "Or should I say, goodbye."

Luke was about to turn into her road. Instead, he put his foot down and continued along the road which led out of town. He said nothing until they reached the open countryside. Then he turned into a side road, and again down a track. He stopped the car.

"Jess, I'm sorry," he said unexpectedly. "You were right. I should never have said those things to you today and I don't blame you for what happened."

Once again, Jess surprised herself. She should have been flooded with happiness, overcome with gratitude that Luke was willing to forgive her outburst. But all she felt was a kind of distant triumph.

"Well, that's big of you," she started to say. But he stopped her.

"No – let me finish. I wanted to say that although I can understand why you reacted like that, I just didn't expect it. It wasn't like you. I didn't recognize you."

Suddenly, as he spoke, Jess felt a flash of understanding. "It's her, isn't it?" she said, surprising herself with her own certainty. He glanced at her.

"What are you talking about?" he demanded. As he spoke, Jess knew her instincts were right.

190

"Imogen," she said softly. "You just couldn't take it when I stood up to you today. Because that's the kind of thing she used to do, isn't it?"

Luke's face darkened with pain as he stared straight ahead. It was beginning to rain, and the windscreen was misting up. Jess knew, without a doubt, that this was the end for them. But instead of feeling sadness, she felt calm and certain. She reached out for Luke's hand and squeezed it.

"I think maybe I'm not the person you wanted me to be," she said gently.

Slowly, he turned to face her. His eyes were tender, and he smiled – the old, charming smile. "Maybe not – but you are a great person, a wonderful person. The sexiest Fairy Godmother who's ever cast a spell on me."

Jess smiled back, suddenly fond of Luke. "You know, in the end you'd have got sick of having a passive, hopeless, clinging female hanging round your neck," she teased him. "I reckon you don't really want someone to dominate, any more than you want to be dominated by the Imogens of the world. Next time, why not go for an equal?" As she spoke, she thought with a pang of Thomas. Already, Luke was beginning to seem far away, like a stranger.

"I guess this is the end for us, isn't it?" he whispered. When she nodded, he squeezed her hand, then started the car and began to drive her home again.

Outside her house, he pulled her towards him and kissed her lips very gently. "I'll never forget you, Jess," he said quietly. "These last few months, with you – it's been great. Hasn't it?"

"It's been like a dream," Jess assured him with a gentle smile. But as she slipped out of the car and made her way to the front door, she was overcome with relief that it was over, it was finally all over. Now she was herself again. And she was free.

Twenty

There was a sudden crack of a whip, the band burst into a country hoedown, and a full-blooded Tennessee twang announced merrily: "Cinderella – you *shall* go to the ball!"

Jess had rehearsed this bit so often that she positively relished her first appearance in the show, slapping her hands on her thighs and beaming heartily at the audience. There was an astonished ripple of laughter. She waited for a few seconds longer than usual, before declaiming: "I am your Fairy Godmother!" When the audience laughed even louder she turned to them indignantly and added a few extra lines of her own.

"Oh, so there's some folk out there don't believe me, huh?" Her scornful eyes swept the packed auditorium. "We-ell, ladies and gentlemen, let me tell y'all a thang or two. I most certainly am a Fairy Godmother, and anyone don't believe me I'll see you outside after the show and we'll have a little shooting contest, shall we?"

Jess could hardly believe that the show was really happening at last. It had only been three months – but they had been the most eventful, the most wonderful, and the most difficult months of her life in so many ways that she felt like a completely different person now. In fact, she felt very different from the person she had been even three days ago: the three days since the Dress Rehearsal.

Nothing much had happened since then, at least, not outwardly. But inside Jess had been going through such a churning turmoil of thoughts and emotions that those three days had felt like a lifetime.

She'd gone to college as usual. As usual she'd snatched a quick lunch in the canteen with Ellie, and listened to the latest instalment of her now budding romance with Max. She hadn't seen Thomas, except for one brief glimpse when she'd been coming out of the Social Studies class and seen him going into the library. Her stomach had flipped at the sight of him. She didn't know whether she was relieved that they hadn't come face to face. Or heartbroken.

"So – have you made it up with Luke?" Ellie demanded, with her usual tact.

"Oh, no," Jess answered with a shrug. "We're definitely

finished. Thank goodness!"

Ellie, who had a sixth sense when it came to romantic attachments, immediately pounced. "There's someone else, isn't there?" She peered closely into her friend's eyes. "You'd never have stood up to Luke before. I knew something must have changed you in a big way."

Jess sighed. "I don't think it's quite as simple as that," she began.

"Oh, for heaven's sake!" Ellie interrupted. "That's you all over, isn't it? How come life is simple for the rest of us, just not you? How come I can say I'm hungry and you have to say you're torn between wanting the sandwich and worrying about whether the ham is fresh and what kind of pickle they used. How come I can say I fancy someone but you have to analyse the difference between infatuation and lust, just fancying or fancying like mad, simple attraction and fatal attraction. Oh, and while we're on the subject, how come I can just say I love someone and you have to ponder on about whether it's really love, or being in love, or falling in love, or just loving like you do a friend . . . ?"

"Well, that's just the point," Jess put in while Ellie took a breath. "It's Thomas."

Ellie fell silent. "Wow," she said. "See your point." She wasn't silent for long, though. "Has anything happened?" she asked eagerly.

Jess shook her head. "Not really. I don't even think he

knows."

Ellie snorted. "You might as well have your head in a bucket, Jessica Mackenzie. Thomas is in love with you. I mean, he loves you. I mean, he's very attracted to you. He thinks you're nice. He oh, what's the point, right first time, he's in love with you. Always has been. It's not complicated, Jess. It's simple."

"How – how do you know?" stammered Jess.

"Well it's obvious," Ellie said pityingly. "To anyone except you, anyhow. Thomas is nuts about you. If you feel the same way you just have to tell him."

After that, Jess floated through the next few days until the first performance of the pantomime. She found herself piecing together all the clues which suddenly began to make sense. The way Thomas always helped to choose her clothes even for dates with Luke. The beautiful brooch he'd given her for her birthday, hidden in that copy of *Sugar* so that no one would guess how he felt about her. His anger at her treatment of Matthew. Could that have been his own jealousy about her? Then she remembered all his acts of kindness. How he'd always helped her out: at school, in the band, during the pantomime when she'd got into such a mess. There was that card he'd sent when she was ill . . . and then the Dress Rehearsal. She relived for the thousandth time the charge that had shot through her when their hands had touched . . .

Luke had not attempted to get in touch with her after they'd agreed to break up. And she hadn't wanted him to. She was amazed at her own calmness. It wasn't as if Luke had changed at all. But she had. And that was why she had been able to stand up to him in that blaze of anger. The spell had finally been broken, and at last she was herself again.

But all that had been set aside on Saturday for the first real performance of the show. Everyone had been in a state of high excitement from early that morning, bustling round the theatre in frantic last-minute panic and getting in each other's way.

"People, people," shouted a harassed Michael Wayne. "Calm down, everyone. Now, if this was the West End, you wouldn't be here at all. You'd be home, asleep, conserving your energy I can remember the last time I played in a pantomime. It was *Alice in Wonderland*. I was Tweedledum and my very good friend Alex was Tweedledee. We were so keen to conserve our energies that we went for a little relaxing drink or two in the very acceptable little watering hole on the corner . . ." He smiled dreamily at the memory, his mood suddenly serene. ". . . very nearly missed our call," he went on. "Nice little thing playing the dormouse had to come and find us . . ."

He remembered where he was and called everyone to

order, glancing anxiously over to where Georgia was busily sewing a few extra buttons on to her jacket. She'd decided that you couldn't ever have enough of them if you were playing Buttons.

She didn't even look up, and Jess noticed that Matthew seemed to be hovering very close. She did a double take. He wasn't just hovering – he was actually sewing a few buttons on himself!

But there was no time for speculation. It was as if all emotional attachments had been put on hold for the day, while everyone concentrated on their one big collective passion. Jess felt a sudden rush of panic when Luke sauntered in. Although she didn't love him any more, she couldn't help feeling sad that their break-up had been so bitter and so very public.

But, much to her relief, he just waved casually at her. Feeling more cheerful, she waved back and grinned. Despite everything, she was fond of him. And then there was suddenly no time to think about anything except the show. She threw herself into practising the transformation of Cinderella one more time. Luke was equally busy, running through the score with the band. Ellie and Max were busy, too – so busy that they showed up rather late, looking flustered and very pleased with themselves. But as soon as they arrived, they too were caught up in the rush of activity and chaos.

"I'm – I'm a bit nervous," whispered Jasmine to Jess. Jess was surprised. Jasmine very rarely confessed to having any feelings at all. She wasn't the sort to admit weaknesses. Jess looked at her closely. She seemed very young suddenly – and vulnerable. Jess gave her a sudden hug.

"You're going to be great!" she said warmly. 'You're a wonderful actress, you know – but I think we'd better do the dress thing one more time, and then the lizards and rats. But don't be too disgusted. I want you to save your best disgust for the afternoon!"

And then the time began to rush by much too fast. The cast had squeezed into their costumes, their faces glistened with grease paint, the theatre was filling up with the screams and chatter of five hundred children and assorted adults. Jess was desperate to peep through the curtain and catch a glimpse of the audience. But Michael had forbidden any of them to do that. He said it brought bad luck.

Now here she was on stage, thoroughly enjoying herself. "HE'S BEHIND YOU!" the children were shrieking in delight. Matthew dodged to her left as she swung round. Then dodged the other way as she swung again. The audience roared and screamed. At last, she managed to turn all the reptiles and rodents into coachmen and horses and turned her attention to Cinderella. She cracked her whip, the stage filled with dry ice as a filmy curtain descended. The band struck up a gentle few bars and Jess sang one haunting verse of the theme song, knowing that behind that curtain Jasmine was frantically scrambling into her ballgown.

It worked! The audience gasped in wonder as the ice receded, the curtain was lifted, and there was Cinderella, sparkling and glittering, ready for the ball. After she'd swept out in her carriage, Jess's heart began to pound again. She'd enjoyed everything so far, but the next scene was the big test. She was alone with Buttons, and they were about to perform the duet that had given her so many nightmares.

"Cheer up, Buttons," she said cheerfully. "Ain't no woman worth that amount of tears. And who knows. If the magic can happen to her, maybe it can happen to you, too." Then she and Georgia linked arms. She glanced down. Georgia was smiling at her. She even managed a wink. The band was urging them into their routine. Suddenly, Jess wasn't on stage in front of a packed audience. She was back in the empty gym. The arm round her waist was Thomas's. The steps were the steps he'd taught her. Before she knew it the song and dance were over, the audience was cheering:

"We've never done it that well," Georgia was whispering triumphantly in her ears.

As the curtain fell for the end of Act One, Jess found herself tripping backstage, straight into the arms of Thomas. He'd been standing in the wings waiting for her, his face rouged and spattered with beauty spots, a cascade of bright red hair coiled into a beehive, his purple and yellow gown plumped up with pillows. He towered over her thanks to his ten-centimetre stilettos.

"I told you you'd be fine," he said, holding her arms as if to steady her. Jess knew with sudden clarity that she didn't want him to let go.

"I had to pretend it was you up there," she whispered. "That's what made it OK." For another long moment they stared into each other's eyes, oblivious to the bustle going on around them. Their faces moved closer together, very slowly. Jess was willing him with all her might to kiss her. But as his lips were about to touch hers he suddenly pulled away.

"What can I be thinking of?" he squawked in his Ugly Sister voice. "It would just ruin my make-up and heaven knows that would never do!"

They all sailed through the rest of the show. Everyone seemed to be on a high as they realized how all the drudgery, the hard work, the repetitive grind of rehearsals was now paying off. There was a wonderful feeling of togetherness as they all gathered on stage for the final number.

"And if you – if you truly believe
Then one day, one day,
One day it will happen to you!"

Jess, at the front of the stage, hand in hand with Jasmine and Georgia, could just about glimpse Ellie and Max, side by side in the orchestra pit, their eyes locked as they played the familiar strains. There were Ben and Molly, clapping in time in the front row. It was almost as if the song was coming true.

When they had taken their final curtain call, to tumultuous cheers and screams of applause, they all crowded into the wings, hugging each other and kissing their congratulations.

"Well done, chaps," Michael effused, passing everyone glasses of champagne and orange juice. "I knew you'd pull out all the stops." He looked a little awkward as he handed Georgia her glass, but she just smiled, and kissed him lightly on the cheek before turning away to someone standing right behind her. Jess could barely prevent herself from gawping. Because the person with Georgia, putting his arm protectively round her shoulders, was Matthew. And as Georgia turned to him, Jess caught a glimpse of her face, transformed, shining with happiness.

"Whoever would have thought it," said a familiar voice behind her. "Love's young dream, just where you wouldn't have expected it." It was Luke, grinning his most sardonic grin. Then he added, more seriously: "You sang like an angel tonight."

Once again, Jess was astonished to find that she was able to hear that voice, see that face, without the slightest affect. "Glad to see you finally took my advice about toning it down for the duet," he added. She just smiled – a friendly, no-hard-feelings sort of smile, and he ruffled her hair in a big-brotherly gesture. "Fancy coming out for dinner?" he added. "I was thinking of the tapas bar . . ."

Ellie tugged her arm. "We're all going for a pizza at The Park Inn," she said. "Coming?"

"OK," Jess answered, flashing Luke a rueful smile. He shrugged, and left.

In the crowded dressing-room she quickly changed back into her jeans and boots and was scrubbing at the last remnants of greasepaint when Thomas appeared in the doorway, looking rather pale.

"That blusher just isn't working for you," she remarked lightly as she joined him.

"I've decided to go for the natural look," he answered. But he wasn't smiling, and his voice sounded strained. They made their way out of the theatre in silence. By the time they reached the street Jess knew he was waiting for a signal from her. So she slipped her hand into his.

"Jess!" he began. Then she was in his arms and at last his

lips found hers and he was kissing her with an intensity that made her senses reel. Ellie and Max sauntered by arm in arm, followed by Ben and Molly, Jasmine, Matthew – the whole crowd. And still Thomas was holding her as though he would never let her go. Gazing wonderingly into each other's eyes, barely able to take in what was happening to them, they were locked, for that moment, in a perfect fusion of passion and tenderness. And somehow, cradled in his warmth, her whole being melting into his embrace, Jess knew that she'd finally come home where she belonged.